Other Buck Logan Suspense Novels by
J.R. Stoddard

COUGAR CAMP

To Luke

Enjoy

Happy Hunting

J.R. Stoddard

Thought you might
like this!
Love
From mom

COUGAR HUNT

By

J.R. STODDARD

A Buck Logan Suspense Novel

Cougar Publishing

THIS IS A J. R. STODDARD BOOK

Copyright April 2000 by J. R. Stoddard
ISBN: 0-9701401-0-X

COUGAR HUNT. Copyright @ 2000 by J. R. Stoddard.
Second Printing July 2005

FIRST EDITION

Cover Designed by Kathy Campbell
The sixteen cougar pictures and one bear picture in this book are original photos taken by Lee Drygert

---

Stoddard, Jerry R., 1946-

Cougar Publishing
Olympia, Washington

J. R. STODDARD

Dedicated to my loving wife and best friend Carolyn
and our three wonderful children Susan, Eric and Robert

Acknowledgements

I would like to thank the following people for their help in making this book a reality: Carolyn, my loving wife for twenty-seven years, for all her proofreading and great ideas. Mary Baker, Geri Maynard, Barbara Maynard, Robert Maynard, and Bob Hill for proofreading and providing insight to add new dimensions to the story and the characters. Lee Dygert for his great cougar and bear pictures.

Throughout life we rarely take the time to reflect on the positive impact others have on our lives. This is particularly true for the teachers we have had during our educational years.   As a past teacher I know their efforts are almost always intangible.   I would like to take this opportunity to express my gratitude to those who have had a dynamic impact on my life.

I would like to thank my parents for all the camping, fishing and hunting experiences they gave me while growing up and for giving me a love of nature. These experiences gave me an understanding of the wild and provided me with much of the basis for this novel.

I would also like to thank my college professors from California State University, Fullerton; Eric Hanauer, for getting me off on my life's career on the right foot, Dr. Eula Stovall for her sage council, and Dr. Elmer Johnson for his advice in writing my masters thesis.

Photo by Lee Dygert

1

Buck Logan wheeled down the street in his forest green 1997 Dodge Stealth. Buck, a recently retired Naval aviator, appreciated the intricacies of a fine tuned, powerful machine. Sleek and fast, and in some ways, if one stretched the imagination it was similar to flying a high powered jet aircraft, only it operated in a two dimensional environment as opposed to the three dimensional environment of a jet. As he drove past the sporting goods store he realized he still needed to replace the flint and magnesium match for his survival pack he'd lost on the last fieldtrip. He wheeled into the parking lot and cruised back to the sporting goods store.

The store was huge inside, in line with the latest concept in retail stores. Whoever had the biggest store was the winner. He found a store employee and asked, "Where would I find a flint and magnesium match?"

The employee, Steven Long, led him to the camping section. There was only one choice so that made it easy.

Buck asked, "What about solar blankets? Where would I find those?"

"What do you need it for?"

"I'll use it for an outdoor education class I teach at the university and for a one week course for the local school district. I'll also keep it in a pack that I carry around when hiking or fishing. You never know when you might need one around here," Buck replied.

"I recommend a plain blue plastic tarp and an extra large, heavy duty plastic trash bag or two. The film type blanket will tear or come apart at the seams after about one year, they just don't last very long. The trash bags will last for years and will keep the water out. If you put a hole in the bottom of it, you can pull it on over your head and use it as a poncho, it'll keep you warm and dry too. The tarp is also very versatile and can come in handy at times. Neither one will take up very much space in your backpack, and they're both inexpensive."

"Hey thanks, that's some good information. You never know when you're going to learn something new. You're right about the solar blankets, they only last about a year. I appreciate it. Where are the tarps located?"

"They're on aisle fifteen, about half way down the aisle, on the right side."

He paid for the metal match and two small tarps and returned to his favorite toy, the next best thing to an airplane. It may not break the sound barrier, but it sure could fly down the highway. 'Kick the tires and light the fires.' He got in and fired it up. The stealthy purr got his adrenaline pumping. He whipped into the traffic, entered the freeway, and let it fly.

By the time Steven Long finally got off work he was really irritated. He had to work past his scheduled work time again today. It was turning into a regular event already, and he'd only worked there for two weeks. This new job may not work out the way he had planned. Recently he took the job at the sporting goods store because it fit into his workout schedule. He told them at the interview he only wanted to work twenty hours a week. Since the day he started, either someone didn't show up for work or they showed up late and he was pressured into working after his scheduled end time to cover for the no shows. Now his workout was going to start late and he may not finish before dark. To make matters worse the traffic was stopped, pushing his workout back even more.

Steven was a triathlon athlete. The triathlon is three events; swimming, biking, and running. The race starts with swimming point nine-three miles then goes to bicycling for twenty-four point eight six miles, and then to a run of six point two-one miles. The next scheduled meet was in Hawaii on April 16, 2000, and he needed to place in the top ten to maintain his slot as the Olympic hopeful. So far he had a very limited sponsorship of shoes and some running clothes, but no travel money. Travel was expensive, airfare and hotels atc up a big part of his meager income. He could live on a minimal amount of money as long as he was able to stay in the top ten of the competitors for the event. The apartment in Newtown was an efficiency and his car was an old beater, but reliable. He didn't have time for a girlfriend, in fact, he didn't really have many friends at all.

The location of his apartment was not perfect, but it was acceptable. A nearly new and well-maintained fifty-meter pool was only a block away from his new job and most of the time he could get a lane to himself. He worked out a deal with the coach of a swim team that leased the pool so he could workout for a nominal price anytime he could get to the pool, depending on his work schedule. It worked well because, as it turned out, his work schedule was always changing. There were many good bicycle-racing courses within five miles. Running was a different matter, places to run were everywhere, but finding challenging courses took time. Each place he competed presented a different challenge. Hawaii is a hot, humid climate and that's hard to train for in the northwest. He decided a higher elevation run would help compensate for the temperature difference.

He found a great place to run only fifteen minutes from his apartment in a National Forest area at an elevation of three thousand five hundred feet. Running at this elevation gave him an extra advantage because the air was thinner, less oxygen, because the pressure density was less. It made it harder to run and gave him a more intense workout. Since it was higher and harder, he usually only ran ten miles for each workout. The whole workout time would be a little less than two hours, including warm up and cool down time. He would be pushing the time limit tonight. Running after dark could be a problem since he couldn't see as well. Stepping wrong on a rock, or in a rut, a hole or anything that could twist an ankle, would be bad news. Anything that kept him from working out would keep him out of the top ten and make it harder for him to come back at the next meet to re-gain his Olympic hopeful slot.

After sitting in stop and go traffic he finally got home from work. He quickly changed into his running clothes, and on his way out grabbed three water bottles and three high-energy power bars and was on his way out the door. Evening twilight was around seven o'clock so he'd have to push it to complete his workout before dark. He'd been running the National Forest trail at Cross Point for over a year now and it was his favorite place to run. Eating the power bars as he drove to the site he went over his route in his head.

At five fifteen he brought the car to a stop in the same place he always parked. It was obvious other people had been there, but he had never seen anyone else in the time he'd been running there. Actually he found comfort in the solitude. It was a beautiful spring evening. The leaves were coming out on the trees. In addition to the many evergreen trees in the forest there were many deciduous trees, such as alder, maple, and even a few oaks. The evergreen trees were putting out their incredible spring scent. Steven could physically feel the stress flow out his body.

As he began stretching and doing some warm-up exercises he could hear the birds singing from all directions. While he was taking a big drink from a water bottle, he heard a different sound, a strange sound that he had only noticed once or twice before. It was a sort of a low growl followed be a short hiss. He'd heard it when he was up here before, but he couldn't quite picture what was making the strange sound. Maybe it was from the Discovery Channel as he tried to remember the sound. Whatever it was, it sent a chill down his spine. Finished with the stretching he strapped on a waist pack with two water bottles and took a quick look around. Noticing nothing out of the ordinary, he was anxious to get going.

It felt good to be on the familiar gravel road at a comfortable pace. The trail in the center of the road was in good condition, but was somewhat overgrown along the edges. There were obviously other people, or animals using the trail too. It had once been a logging road, but was no longer wide enough for even an SUV to use. There was a beautiful forest on both sides of the road at the beginning of the run. The trees were very old and the branches from each side of the road grew together to create an arching canopy. The trail was flat for about five hundred yards and then went into a slight decline.

Steven had been running for about fifteen minutes. As he ran down the forest trail it came to a meadow. Of all the courses he had run over the years, this was his favorite place, it was mystical. There was a stream going through the middle of the meadow, with huge trees around the perimeter, and it looked just like a travel brochure. Back when he first started running there, in the early morning or evening, there were almost always deer present and he frequently saw raccoons, foxes, coyotes, and even elk. He always thought it was a special place, but lately it had been different. As he jogged he realized that he hadn't seen the usual forest activity for nearly two months. He thought perhaps it's just the time of the year, or maybe the animals had moved on to some other area in search of a new food source. Now he wasn't so sure.

Along the service road were trees that were hundreds of years old. In one of the old spruce trees lay a cougar, the most voracious predator in North America. The mother cougar was looking for food to feed her offspring who were asleep in the woods nearby. She was stretched out on a branch directly over the intersection of a game trail and the service road, a strategic location. She had spent most of her life in the general area and she now had five kittens to feed. They were almost ready to go out on their own, but two of the five were undernourished.

The mother cougar watched intently as Steven ran along the service road. She'd watched Steven run in the same area before, mostly with curiosity. She had been in this very same tree many times as Steven ran right under her. As usual, she watched, but this time she was more focused, watching his every move, this time was different.

She was very hungry and had to feed her hungry offspring.

She'd given birth to six kittens eighteen months ago. Cougars usually give birth to two or three kittens, a litter of six kittens is very unusual. When there is an abundance of food, animals have larger and more frequent litters. Eighteen months ago there had been an abundance of deer, as there had been for many years before that. However, as the deer population diminished, there were too many cougars in the area to survive on the amount of game left. One of the kittens had died shortly after it was born. The mother cougar sensed that her remaining kittens would soon be dispersed to be on their own and fend for themselves. Two kittens were malnourished because of the diminishing food supply. They had not eaten for weeks.

Cougars are carnivores. They like fresh meat, and sometimes will eat prey while it is still alive. At five years old the mother cougar weighed in at one hundred twenty pounds. Less than Steven, at one hundred fifty-five pounds, but there was a big difference, a cat is pure muscle. A hundred twenty pound cougar can carry a hundred-pound prey for great distances. In fact, a cougar can jump up a cliff or over a six foot high fence, while carrying a hundred-pound prey.

The cougar's primary source of food is deer. An adult cougar has a voracious appetite and can sometimes eat twenty to thirty pounds of meat at a single feeding when sufficiently hungry. One cougar will usually kill a deer about every seven days, depending on the availability. With six cougars, the mother and her five kittens, one deer was barely enough to feed them for one meal. In the past year the mother and kittens had systematically reduced the deer population to nearly zero in her roaming area. For the past two months the cougar and her kittens had existed on rabbits, raccoons and mice.

Their last meal, two weeks ago, was a skunk. The cougars were famished.

As Steven ran down the trail toward the junction at the end of the meadow, the mother cougar watched intently. This was not its normal prey, but the cougar was desperate, she and her kittens were starving. At this point, any live meat was fair game.

Steven was only half way through his run and he was beginning to sweat heavily. He'd soon start back up the hill at the end of the meadow. It was a nice run, and the weather was perfect. He should easily make it back to the car just before it got too dark.

At the end of the meadow Steven heard that low growl again, it sent a chill up his spine. The source was much closer than it had been before. He slowed down and looked around. Something was not right, and he had an uncomfortable, intuitive feeling, like someone, or something, was watching him. Continuing, but more slowly, as the feeling of doom slowly began to surround him. Suddenly, he felt all alone and vulnerable. Maybe running out here by himself wasn't such a good idea after all. It was such a beautiful place and he hated to think it was changing. He loved it here, but all of a sudden he had a sinking feeling. He pressed on even though his legs began to feel heavy.

The cougar was totally focused on Steven as he passed under the tree. She was hungry and this looked like a meal. The cougar tensed as she continued to watch and wait for about a minute after Steven had passed under the tree. Silently she dropped off her perch fifteen feet, from the ground, and began to stalk Steven, watching intently, his every move. She increased her pace to keep up with the runner.

Steven thought he heard something. It was not much, but it was there. Maybe it was just instinct or a feeling in the back of his head, like a sixth sense. The hair on the back of his neck began to bristle. Suddenly something seemed wrong, very wrong. He slowed and started to turn his head around. There, about twenty feet behind him, he saw the cougar following him.

The cougar quickly stopped and studied the runner. Steven wasn't familiar with cougars or their habits, but he thought it was best to get away from bears as quickly as possible. Maybe cougars were the same. He was a fast runner and figured with the distance now between him and the cougar he could out run it. He gave it all he had.

Fast as lightning the cougar leapt onto Steven's back. He was ready for it and spun around, elbowing the cougar in the side and knocked it off of him. Giving the cougar a swift kick in the side, knocking it off balance as it retreated. This might have been enough to discourage most cougars if he had stood his ground and stared it down making threatening gestures.

Thinking he could get away, Steven began to run again. The cougar took three steps and jumped twenty feet onto Steven's back. This time it sunk its razor sharp front claws into Steven's shoulders and its rear claws into his lower legs. At the same time the cougar clamped its massive jaws into the back of Steven's neck.

Steven felt the shock of the cougar landing full force on his back again, a searing pain raced through his back, legs, and the back of his head. The attack caused him to fall forward. He put his hands in front of him to break his fall and twisted his wrist.

The cougar pulled its claws down Steven's back and pushed its hind legs down at the same time. She ripped huge gashes down Steven's back and legs and caused massive bleeding. Steven was in excellent physical condition and he rolled over with what strength he had left trying to dislodge the cat. Even an athlete in top physical condition is no match for a cougar if it is starving. The cougar was partly dislodged but recovered fast. Lurching forward, she quickly clamped her jaws on Steven's throat. Steven's eyes bulged out in horror as he tried to scream, but his throat was sealed shut. He stabbed his thumb and index finger into the cougar's eyes and tried to force it off of him, but the cougar twisted her head violently from side to side, breaking his neck.

The cougar dragged the body up a trail and into the woods. Dragging a human body was easy compared to dragging an elk or a large deer. She dragged the body along the trail until she reached a clearing. Her five offspring were sleeping in the trees around the clearing. They awoke immediately, dropping out of the trees and began to investigate. Soon they began clawing at the clothing, tearing away his cloths and ripping large gashes in his tender flesh.

Two of the healthiest kittens snarled at the two weaker, unhealthy kittens, forcing them to back off and wait until the others had finished eating. The fifth kitten was healthy but didn't want to fight so it backed off and waited until the two aggressive ones left. One hungry cougar can eat up to thirty pounds of meat at a single feeding.   Within hours, the six hungry cougars easily devoured Steven.   When they were done there was nothing left but a skeleton, and blood soaked running clothes and shoes, one of which still contained a foot. In a situation like this a lone person in the woods could easily disappear without a trace. Even large search parties that went on for days, might not find the remains.

When the mother cougar killed Steven Long, she changed the feeding instinct of her offspring.   Humans were no longer to be feared and avoided. They were now food.

The next afternoon, as the rest of the cougar family slept, the two healthiest kittens, a male and a female, went out to hunt together. They headed south in the general direction of Newtown.   In their search for food, they left the National Forest area and entered a huge tree farm that belonged to Walter Johnson.

In the early evening, as they slowly moved through the forest, they heard a noise. It sounded like a rake being dragged down the bark of a tree. They both stopped and listened intently.   They spotted a raccoon coming down a tree for its evening search for food.   Slowly they began to move in the direction of the tree.

The raccoon reached the ground and began sniffing around.   As it worked its way toward a small stream the cougars stealthily moved in closer.   When they were about thirty feet away the male kitten took off at a full run for the raccoon.   Sensing danger, it looked around to see the cougar moving in for an attack.   It headed back up the tree as fast as it could.   From twenty feet away the cougar jumped, landing ten feet up the tree, right next to the raccoon.   He quickly grabbed the raccoon in his massive jaws and clamped down hard enough to snap its spine. He brought the meal back down the tree and began tearing it apart.   The female kitten came over and tried to get her share, but the male wasn't in the mood to share and chased her off.

Photo by Lee Dygert

2

Buck Logan taught an outdoor education and survival class at a nearby university. During his twenty years as a Naval Aviator he attended one-week survival training courses about every three years and he used the experience as the basis for his classes. The Navy courses were different each time, but the first day always started with an aircraft ditching-at-sea scenario. There were numerous different types of survival circumstances and each course proved to be both educational and entertaining. One of the courses he remembered distinctly, one that he would not care to repeat, was called SERE (Survival, Evasion, Resistance and Escape) training. This course was designed as an aircraft crash in hostile territory. Each person traveled alone through a series of escape and evasion tactics. Everyone was eventually caught by the unfriendly forces and taken through a rather unpleasant sequence of interrogations and incarceration. It was great training if one was shot down in enemy territory, but was not appropriate as a part of his university course.

It was eight a.m. Friday morning, the day of the field trip. Buck assembled the class in the university parking lot and had each person lay out the contents of their pack in front of them. He inspected each person's gear for the essential equipment and also to ensure that no contraband was being taken, such as alcohol or drugs. Illegal drugs posed a serious safety hazard to all students during this three-day trip and Buck took a hard stand here. Any illegal drugs resulted in immediate dismissal from the class and the student was turned over to the campus police. Since they're all college students one never knows what might end up in the pack. Any student who didn't have the minimum required equipment was not allowed to go on the field trip. In spite of numerous discussions about the required equipment, one person always showed up with a critical item missing. This time it was Sharon, who had brought a sleeping bag that was not much more than a blanket and was only suitable for use indoors.

Buck told her, "We have some time left before the bus is ready to leave. I'll give you fifteen minutes to come up with a bag that's acceptable. If you can't, you won't be able to go."

Sharon bolted for the dormitory and returned in about ten minutes with a sleeping bag from a friend. Buck inspected it and said it should keep her warm enough for the trip.

The class was not intended to be a real survival situation so everyone brought their own eating utensils and food, usually freeze-dried backpacker's food. The class was offered on a pass or no pass basis and successful completion of the three-day field trip was a requirement to receive a passing grade.

The class was offered through the recreation department, which offered a number of interesting and uniquely different types of experiences that were directly related to life in today's world. Due to safety concerns, Buck could only allow fifteen students per class. The class was wildly over subscribed, with over two hundred students who wanted to take the class every quarter. It was a fun class to teach and he enjoyed the interaction with the university students, but it was exhausting and the pay was so poor he would only teach one class per quarter. Buck couldn't understand the system, it required a master's degree to qualify for a teaching position at the university, but the pay was less than a high school graduate's first job. Something was dramatically wrong with the educational system.

The students loaded all their equipment on the bus and Buck took a head count and assigned each student a number from one to fifteen. Each person would keep the number for the whole trip. It was a quick way to determine if everyone was present so he had them do a practice run.

"When I say 'count off' the person who is number one say 'one' loudly, then 'two' etc. This procedure will be important in the next three days, so don't forget your number."

The field trip required Buck to do substantial planning beforehand. The class went on a bus together to the departure site in the National Forest a little over two hours from the university. From the drop off point the class would hike about four hours to a remote site for the survival experience. Buck had previously positioned a van with survival equipment, extra first aid supplies, a two way radio to the school security office and a spare cell phone, less than one thousand yards from the primary survival site. In addition, the forest service and the closest emergency services department were appraised of their position and schedule.

At ten fifteen they were on their way to a new adventure and everyone was excited. Buck used the bus ride to go over the chain of events in his mind. The school quarter was ten weeks long, but Buck modified the usual class schedule because of the three-day survival experience at the end of the class. The class was given once a week for three hours at a time for the first six weeks of the quarter. At the end of the seventh week the students went on a three-day field trip for practical experience in a nearby national forest. This was always done on Friday, Saturday and Sunday. It was convenient for the students because the eighth week of the quarter was study time for most students to get ready for finals, and that was the week following the field trip. The field trip experience was exhausting and took its toll on everyone.

The first class was spent getting to know everyone, introductions, university major, hobbies, likes and dislikes, etc. Since everyone would be spending three days together, in a potentially stressful environment, teamwork was essential. Buck enjoyed combining the many and varied students together in a cooperative effort. It was a real challenge because every class consisted of the meek and the very aggressive. For the remainder of the class Buck gave an overview of what the class was all about, a schedule of the events and equipment requirements for the field trip.

During the second week, the class discussed environment and how the environment would, initially, be the most important part of a survival experience. It's critical to protect against hypothermia in the northwest, but every real life situation would be different. Hot, cold, wet, or dry, one must be prepared for any situation and understand what to do in each. Protecting oneself against the environment, how and where to find water, and basic first aid. First aid was the only prerequisite to take the class.

Learning how to use a compass and a map was during the third week. This was more challenging than most of the students imagined. Buck spent an hour in the classroom explaining the compass and how it worked. He then took them outside and walked them through a series of exercises he had developed himself. The exercises were designed as a game to make the learning experience more fun and easier to understand. It took the full three hours and it was rare for a student to fully master the art of orienteering. Most of the students could understand the basics by the end of the day and they would get more practical application on the field trip.

Survival, the most important class, was taught the fourth week. The class was spent on the psychology of survival, how and where to find food, what is edible and what is not, and how to test the edibility of potential food sources. Maintaining a positive frame of mind in a survival situation was essential to the experience, whether it be a class or a real life situation. Surprisingly, there are edible food sources around us all the time, but most people don't think about the plants we see every day as being edible. This may actually be good because some of them were poisonous, some could cause a potentially fatal reaction. In a survival situation, one must be able to tell the difference.

The fifth week the class covered habitat. Shelter building was an important element for survival because the environment and availability of materials in the area determined the type of shelter to be constructed. The shelter may be built of sticks, logs, branches, stones, snow, ice, or if one came prepared, a tarp, sleeping bag and a hammock.

The sixth week, the final class before the field trip, was for review and a check of each person's field trip pack. Each class member was required to bring a suitable backpack with the minimum essentials to participate in the trip. The minimums in the pack included a sleeping bag (suitable for temperatures down to 30 degrees), matches, a butane lighter, a knife, rope, a 6x8 foot tarp, two sixteen ounce water bottles, water purification tablets, long underwear, compass, a rain coat or poncho, food, a playground whistle, and eating utensils.

On the way to the drop-off site the road was blocked by an automobile accident. The accident delayed their arrival to the National Forest drop-off site by thirty minutes. It was almost one o'clock when they disembarked the bus. They'd all eaten the lunch they brought with them during the bus ride to avoid loosing any valuable daylight hiking time to the site. Buck had each student take out their map and orient themselves to determine which direction they would head out to the survival site. He organized the students and checked each pack arrangement, then assigned number one to be the first leader. The students would take turns of thirty minutes each leading the group by using the map and a compass. The hike was relatively easy because of the many and varied abilities of the students. It began at an elevation of about fifteen hundred feet and ended at an elevation of two thousand feet.

One hour into the hike the typical northwest weather moved in and it began to rain. Buck stopped the group so everyone could get out their poncho or raincoat. The students were all accustomed to doing things in the rain so they took it in good stride, but it took its toll on their enthusiasm as they continued.

Two hours into the hike Buck took another head count, "Count off."

"One, two, three, four, five, six, seven, eight, nine, ten, eleven."

Buck looked around and quickly realized they were short. "Number twelve, are you here?" How about thirteen?"

"Thirteen, fourteen."

As they hiked Buck made a mental head count about every ten to fifteen minutes and had a 'count off' head count about once per hour. He quickly counted thirteen present. Number twelve and fifteen were missing. Jane and Bill, interesting he thought, they had been particularly chummy throughout the classes. They couldn't be far behind, since he did a mental count less than ten minutes ago.

"This is a good time for a bushes break, men to the left, women to the right. Everyone group up right here afterward. Number three you're the trail leader now, you're in charge until I get back. I'm going to backtrack a little to see what's happened to Jane and Bill."

After about five minutes of backtracking Buck could hear a commotion and heavy breathing in the bushes up the side of the hill. He took off his pack and laid it down on the trail and made himself comfortable. As they emerged from the bushes they saw Buck waiting. Their smiles quickly turned to sheepish red faces.

"I hope we haven't inconvenienced you."

Embarrassed, Bill responded, "Well ah."

"Never mind, just don't do it again."

Their faces were still red when they rejoined the rest of the class. It didn't take long for the group to figure out the likely cause of their delay, but they were thankful for the rest so there were no comments.

"Load up, let's go."

As they got moving along the trail Buck said, "Count off. One, two, … fifteen, that's good. Let's stay on the trail and stay together from now on. If you need a break let me know."

An hour later Kenna twisted her ankle on a tree root growing across the trail. This injected more realism into the experience. Buck inspected the injury, wrapped it and used an inflatable cast to immobilize the ankle. He carried inflatable knee and ankle casts for such emergencies, twisted ankles were not unusual and they were close to their first night survival site now. One of the guys took her pack for her and two of the women assisted her in walking by supporting her on each side. By the time they reached the site everyone was exhausted, cold and wet. The students were accustomed to carrying their books in backpacks that usually weighed around twenty pounds. Most of the backpacks they were carrying today weighed thirty pounds or more. The extra weight and four hours of hiking time made for some weary travelers even in good weather.

Buck tried to time their arrival at the survival site between three and four in the afternoon. Depending on the time of year, there may not be much daylight left by the time they got there. This was a realistic situation for someone lost in the woods, with little time left before dark to set up for an overnight stay. The timing for the day's events would normally give them enough time for about one hour of instruction on arrival to the site and at least one hour left to set up a shelter for the night. It was now after five and the clouds and rain had already hastened the darkness. Between Bill and Jane's foray and Kenna's ankle they were well behind his planned arrival schedule. The fact that everybody was soaking wet made the situation even less fun, but it also made things more realistic for an actual survival situation.

Before Buck had brought his first class to the site, he had spent weeks thinking of every possible adverse scenario. He was prepared for almost anything.

"One, two, three and four go gather some rocks for a fire pit. Fourteen and fifteen stand right here for a reference point for them. Don't loose site of fourteen and fifteen while you are looking for the rocks. Bring the rocks back and make a four-foot diameter fire ring right here. The rest of you come with me."

Buck led them into the woods where he kept a stash of supplies for the camp. He pulled an old parachute out of a box and gave it to three of them and told the others to grab an armload of firewood from the pile. Back at the site Buck showed them how to tie a rope to the top of the canopy and then he threw the rope over a branch in the tree above them and hauled it up about twenty feet off the ground.

"OK, everyone spread out, grab a side and pull the parachute out to the sides in a circle." He handed each student a piece of rope and a stake and told them to secure the edges to a tree or to use a rock to put the stake in the ground and then attach the rope to the stake.

He took a three-foot long branch and propped up a side to use as an entrance and exit opening. In less than thirty minutes, they erected a shelter that could hold all of them for the night. The fire pit was right in the center of the tepee and it was now dark.

"It's too late for us to build individual shelters tonight and I don't want to take a chance on anyone else getting hurt trying to build one in the dark. Grab your backpacks and find yourself a spot inside the shelter for tonight. This arrangement will dry us out and make things more comfortable for the night."

Buck went inside and used his flashlight to show the way, as the students all filed into the tepee and got comfortable inside.

"Next we need a fire. Everyone take a piece of the firewood and start whittling off some kindling. Be careful with the knife, we don't want anyone slicing off any body parts, yours or your neighbors. We don't need any more injuries today."

Buck got a piece of steel wool out of his pack, his flint and magnesium match and his knife. The students placed the fine pieces of wood shavings on the fluffed-up steel wool and got the kindling ready.

"OK, watch closely because this goes fast."

He gave the flint and magnesium and a knife to a student and instructed her to place the butt of the steel at the base of the steel wool and strike the flint with the blade of the knife. The spark hit the steel wool on the first strike and Buck began blowing on the spark. In less than two seconds the wool was flaming and igniting the wood shavings. The students added more kindling and Buck put two softball-sized pinecones in the growing fire. Even though the pinecones were damp the pitch acted as a natural fuel and the fire was going strong in no time.

Buck showed the students how to tie ropes across the upper area of the tepee and they hung their wet clothes up to dry. With the fire and the sixteen people inside it warmed up fast. Buck checked Kenna's ankle and it looked fine, no swelling and not much pain. He took out a cold pack and twisted the bag to activate the chemicals. It immediately became cold and he it applied it to her ankle to increase the odds that it would be OK by tomorrow. By the time they had made dinner and cleaned up, it was nine o'clock and everyone was ready to turn in for the night.

As the group settled down for the night, the fatigue of the day's hike became apparent. Quiet fell on the inside of the tepee, revealing the many and varied sounds of the forest. The sounds were coming from rustling in the bushes, frogs and an assortment of mating calls.

One of the students asked, "What's all that noise?"

"It's almost springtime and it's a nice evening, not too cold and not too hot. It's mating season for most of the animals in the forest, so there should probably be a lot of activity and associated noise in the woods tonight."

Around ten p.m. Mary jumped away from the side of the tent and shrieked. "What's that? Something outside just rubbed against me through the wall of the tent."

Buck shined his flashlight along the side of the tepee. "Most likely it was a raccoon. They're curious and frequently come into campsites at night looking for scraps of food left out by campers. Goodnight again."

At exactly 2 a.m. everyone was awakened by a loud, sharp shriek. It was an eerie sound similar to the scream of a woman being attacked.

"Count off," Buck said as he shined the light around the inside of the tepee.

The response came with all fifteen numbers responding, everyone was accounted for. Just after fifteen sounded off, the spine-chilling shriek came again, it sounded close. They all looked around in the dark searching for an answer, searching for reassurance and security.

Buck lay there in silence waiting for the next terrifying call, knowing it would not be long, since they usually came in threes. He wasn't disappointed as the next call came, they were about two minutes apart.

"Anyone know what that sound was?"

Someone answered, "Sounds like a woman being murdered."

"That was the mating call of a female cougar. Really gets your attention, doesn't it? Sounds like it's about a half mile away. Male cougars up to ten miles away can hear the mating call, depending on the atmospheric conditions, wind and temperature. We'll probably be hearing it off and on for the rest of the night. Don't worry, it isn't as close as it sounds."

As the morning sun brought light to the tepee everyone began waking up, stoking the fire and fixing breakfast. In the daylight the students could see that the site had a big open area surrounded by numerous large fallen trees and other natural structures suitable for making a shelter, using the available materials in the area. The tepee was in the center of the open area and there was suitable space for Buck to set up a dome tent for himself tonight, close enough to provide supervision and emergency assistance.

Buck checked Kenna's ankle again. There was no swelling, so he told her to try walking on it and if there is any pain he would leave her at the site with a friend, for safety, while they went out on a day hike. She said it felt fine so Buck wrapped the ankle with a short Ace bandage to ensure her foot would still fit in her boot.

"If it starts bothering you while we're hiking today, let me know right away."

Buck had everyone except Kenna load their packs with the minimum needed for survival in case of emergency. This included just the basics; sleeping bag, water, raincoat, tarp or cover, knife and lighter.

Buck gathered the students and explained, "We'll spend the day discussing the surrounding area, searching for food and performing the tests to determine if the potential food source is edible. Take out your maps and find our present position and then look around from there to find our destination, Tower Rock. Someone tell me the bearing to Tower Rock."

John said, "240 degrees."

"Does everyone agree?" No one disagreed. "Good, that's correct. Okay, number seven you're the first leader today, let's go."

As they hiked, Buck talked about the forest, the different types of trees and their likely age based on the diameter of the trunks and the tree species. After thirty minutes Buck stopped the group to change leaders. This was a good place for the talk about edible plants because there was a small meadow that had a wide variety of flora.

Buck asked, "Look around you and tell me what's edible."

No answers came forth so Buck began to explain about the plants in the immediate proximity. "First there is oxalis, better known as the three leaf clover. It's edible as is the Oregon grape right here and the salal. Later in the summer there will be berries on many of the plants. Don't eat berries that are bright colors, like red, or have a waxy coating. If you think a leaf is edible break it first, if it oozes a milky substance, don't eat it. When you find something you think is edible use the four-point test. First, rub some of the substance on the inner part of your arm. The skin on the forearm is sensitive, so if it itches, turns your arm red or swells, don't eat it. Second, place a small amount in your mouth for about ten seconds and then take it out. If it tastes bad, puckers your mouth, causes swelling in your mouth or throat, increases your heart rate or any other adverse reaction, don't eat it. Third, put some in your mouth and chew on it for about five seconds and then spit it out. Once again, if it tastes bad, puckers your mouth, increases your heart rate, causes swelling in your mouth or throat or any other adverse reaction, don't eat it. The fourth test is to eat a small amount. After each test wait approximately fifteen minutes and look for adverse reactions before going on to the next test. You should always know any plants in the area that are deadly poisonous, such as the oleander and rhododendron, so that you don't attempt to eat them. Also never eat mushrooms in a survival situation, even if you know the mushroom types. It's not worth the risk and they basically have no nutritional value. Number eight, you're the new leader, let's go."

When they reached the base of Tower Rock they stopped for a rest. Buck looked around.

"Anyone see anything of interest here?"

No one saw what Buck was looking at. "Look in the damp sand here. See the tracks? These are cougar tracks, perhaps the one we heard last night. There are also deer tracks in the sand. Cougars are normally very shy and elusive animals. Until a few years ago people just never saw them, but there's been a disturbing trend in the last few years of cougars showing up in people's backyards in city areas that border forests. This shouldn't be happening because it means that cougars are loosing their fear of humans. If, in fact, this is what's actually happening, it's a very dangerous trend. Cougars are different than bears, if we run into a bear on the trail we want to get away from it. Bears will chase people, but usually it's because of territorial protection. They normally don't chase people very far because they just want you to leave their area. They can be fierce protectors when they have cubs. Stay clear of them, they are not friendly."

"With cougars it's different, don't run or bend over. Make yourself look as big as possible, huddle together into a tight group, wave your arms and make threatening gestures. More importantly, look directly into the cougar's eyes. Case studies have shown that looking into the cougar's eyes establishes dominance and will almost always cause the cougar to leave. But, if they are loosing their fear of humans, the rules may be changing. Be prepared for an attack, and if it does fight vigorously. If you have a knife, get it out and be ready to stab it in the neck or face, go for the eyes if you can. Don't be afraid to hurt it, if it has attacked you it intends to eat you. If you run away it triggers the cougar's instinct to chase its prey. If you bend over or kneel it is a sign of submission. Cougars are very powerful animals, they may look friendly and cuddly, but they're not. They're always looking for something to eat, and they only eat meat."

"You mean they eat people?"

"Up until 1993 cougar incidents were not very common, but since then there has been an increasing number of attacks which resulted in death."

John said, "That's a comforting thought," as he nervously looked around.

When the group arrived back at the survival site, Buck selected a few students to take down the tepee and return it to the storage box. Then he gave the class a break to rest and make lunch. Most of them stretched out on the ground using their packs as a pillow and quickly dozed off. The hike was tiring even with a light pack.

At two-thirty Buck blew his whistle to break them away from their dreams.

"Time to get to work on your survival site for the night. If you look around the perimeter of the clearing area we are in you'll find numerous potential sites to build a shelter. Break up into groups of one to four and go to work. It's now two-thirty, at four thirty we will gather and critique each site. After the critique you'll have about thirty more minutes to do final touch up work on your site before dark. Use the building materials in the area but remember do not cut down or use anything that is still alive. In a real life situation, you'd use anything you find to help you survive, but since we're a class in the National Forest we want to do as little damage as possible. There's plenty of usable materials laying on the ground."

Buck walked around from site to site giving them helpful hints on how to make it more comfortable and how to keep warm and dry inside. There were logs laying around the area and an abundance of branches, moss, and ferns for sealing the weather out.

After dinner, as they sat around the campfire, Buck explained what they should expect for the night and the rules. Anyone in trouble should sound off and let him know. It was a long night. They heard small animals moving around the area and rustling through the bushes similar to the night before, but this time they were in small groups. There's safety in numbers. They felt more comfortable. The night passed without incident. Apparently the cougar found a mate because the unsettling screeching of the previous night was absent. The students were glad they didn't have to listen to that again. It would have been even less fun in the small shelters without the psychological support of greater numbers.

The next morning Buck got everyone up at seven, assigned three people to make a campfire and got the students organized for the events of the day. Buck had the students disassemble all of their shelters after breakfast so the site would be ready for the next class. At ten o'clock the group departed the site to rendezvous with their retrieval bus. The pick-up site was a different place from where they were dropped off. This required the students to use the maps once again and chart a new bearing. As usual, the students took turns at thirty-minute intervals leading the group to the pick-up point using the map and compass.

The first three hours of the hike the students enjoyed the scenery and were glad to be on their way to the end of their journey. They chatted and some of them took pictures to remember their experience. One of the students, John, really enjoyed the trip and all the nature experiences. He left the trail to look over the cliff and get a picture for his trip scrapbook. As he stood on the ledge the ground at the edge of the overhang gave way, sending him down a thirty-foot drop. He crashed into a tree trunk and yelled out in pain getting the group's attention.

They all turned around and headed for the edge to see what had happened. As the group gathered and looked over the edge Buck cautioned them not to follow John's lead. He appraised the situation and took a rope out of his pack, tied it to a tree trunk, and repelled down to John.

"Where does it hurt?"

"My leg."

Buck felt around and figured it was probably broken, fortunately, not a compound fracture. That would have made the situation much worse.

"Any place else particularly painful?"

"No, just my leg."

Buck had him move his arms, one at a time and then his good leg, head and neck to ensure there was no spinal injury.

He called up to the group, "Looks like he has a broken leg. Bill, please bring my pack down here. Put the pack on your back and use the rope to repel down. The rest of you collect three or four branches about one to two inches in diameter so we can make a splint for his leg. We also need two strong branches about three to four inches in diameter and at least seven feet long so we can make a stretcher."

The students quickly went to work searching for the materials they needed. When they had everything they repelled down to the tree with the branches. Buck got two rolls of duct tape out of his pack and had John lay back while he instructed two of the students in making a splint for his leg. He had the students do all the work, it was excellent real life survival experience. He got a plastic tarp out of his pack and had four other students wrap the tarp over the two long carrying branches and tie them to the poles to make the stretcher. When the splint was on and the stretcher ready they moved John to the stretcher. Eight of the students grabbed the sides and Buck stayed behind them as they worked their way slowly back up the hill. Buck held the repelling rope under the stretcher, using his body as a brace to assist in moving John up the hill and also to stop the stretcher from falling down the hill if someone slipped and they dropped him.

When they were safely at the top and back on the trail Buck pulled the cell phone out of his backpack and called the rescue team. He told them they had a student with a probable broken leg, and he was in good shape otherwise. The students would carry the accident victim out to the bus pick-up point and they would meet the medic team there in about forty minutes.

The medic team arrived at the rendezvous site when they appeared up the trail. They took their stretcher up to meet the hikers and quickly evaluated John's condition and transferred him into their care.

"You all did an excellent job taking care of him and getting him out of there. Thanks for the help transporting him out. If we had to go in after him it would've been well after dark by the time we got him back here. Who knows what might have happened carrying him out in the dark."

The bus was also waiting for them when they arrived. It didn't take long for them to load up for the trip home. They were all concerned about John's condition as the rescue vehicle pulled away. It could have easily been any of them on the way to the hospital.

They arrived at the university parking lot at six thirty

Sunday evening exhausted, but much wiser in many ways. It usually took them all about three days to get fully rested after the experience, which is the reason Buck chose to complete the class the week before their finals week got started.

Photo by Lee Dygert

3

Walter Johnson lived on an extensive tree farm that
bordered a large part of the Newtown City limits on the
north side. He was picking weeds in his vegetable garden
on a beautiful March day. The sun was out, which was
remarkable in itself, for a northwest day in March. It
hadn't rained for two days and the temperature was
almost sixty, not that the usual rain would stop Walter
from being outside. He had worked outside in the rain
most of his eighty-five years. These days he was less keen
on working in the rain though, so he took full advantage
of every dry day to get things done outside.

The garden was in good shape for this early in the
season. The cabbage, garlic and onions were growing
great and the broccoli was starting to come up. He
planted carrots and radishes this morning, and potatoes
last week in the rain. He'd plant some peas and string

beans next week. Maude would have the tomatoes growing in the house already if she was still with him. Couldn't put them outside though until after May the fifteenth because there was still a chance of a freeze until then. Even a slight freeze would kill the young tomato plants. The best way to do tomatoes was to get them growing inside in early March and plant them in the garden after May fifteenth. They'd grow like crazy and you would have tomatoes two to three months earlier. Walter needed to get the seeds planted inside soon to get them going.

Walter missed Maude some days more than others, today was one of those days. The vegetable garden had always been her job and she had done a great job of it too. They practically lived off the land for sixty-five years. Between her vegetable garden and him shooting a deer every month or so, they'd eaten well and spent very little money on food. She canned vegetables in the summer and they lasted all winter. After Maude passed away ten years ago, Walter went to the store more often and bought food. He didn't know how to can the vegetables and didn't want to either. Summer was bountiful, but in the winter he bought most of his food.

He bought the two hundred acres of prime timberland for five hundred dollars in 1935. During the depression land was cheap, unemployment was high and nobody had any money. Walter took a very dangerous job as a deck hand on a fishing boat in the ominous northwest winter. He made twenty dollars for one month of work and took it to a poker game that lasted three days. He walked away from the game with five hundred and twenty dollars. The next day he went to a land auction and bought the two hundred acres. No one else bid on the land because it was over thirty miles east of Seattle and in the middle of nowhere. Worse yet, there were very few roads going out there. The roads that were there were nothing but mud ruts. Walter understood the value of the timber. He figured even with depression prices being so low, the wood on the land was worth way over five hundred dollars. All he had to do was find a way to get the logs to the mill.

After Walter acquired the property he used his last twenty dollars to buy a saw and some other tools and transportation out to the property. He managed to build a one-room log cabin. with a dirt floor, on the property from trees he cut down himself. He married Maude that same year, she was a beautiful young woman. Their married life started out hard for them way out there. During the depression, life was hard almost everywhere. They were happy, just the two of them, they had a roof over their head, a warm dry cabin with a wood cooking stove that doubled as a heater for the cabin. Walter supplied all the deer they could eat and she learned to plant a garden. It wasn't long before they were much better off than most of the people who lived in the city.

A few months after their marriage Maude decided she needed a well. She quickly got tired of walking all the way down to the stream every time she needed water. Walter picked a good spot for a well about thirty feet from the house and started digging. When he got the hole about ten feet deep the sides caved in on him and almost buried him alive. Maude had to help dig him out and told him to come up with a better plan before he continued. He went into town and spent some of his hard earned tree harvest money on well casing, loaded it onto his horse drawn wagon and headed home to start over. This time, whenever the hole got deep enough, Maude helped him hoist a section of the interlocking casing into place and push it down around the walls of the hole. The three-foot diameter terra cotta casing kept the sides from caving in on him and would protect the well for many years.

Digging the well was hard work and it took two people to do the job efficiently. Walter at the bottom of the well digging and filling a bucket, and Maude at the top hauling the dirt out in the filled bucket. She'd dump the bucket and send it back down. It was backbreaking hard work for both of them. Deep in thought Walter remembered one day when the well was about twenty feet deep, Maude didn't have enough strength left to pull him out when he was finished digging for the day. He sat at the bottom of the well for over an hour before he came up with an idea. He told her to go get one of the horses and a rope and she was finally able to pull him out. This revelation started a whole new era for them.

The next day he built the first of many tri-pods over the well. He rigged a pulley system at the top and used the horse to lower and raise himself as well as bring up the buckets of dirt. Maude was so overjoyed at this invention she danced and sang all day that first day they put it into use.

He hit water when the hole was about thirty feet deep. The bottom of the well had to be at least five feet below the water level in order to be able to dip the water out with a bucket, and get clean, silt free water. This was when the really hard part started. The water was cold, about fifty degrees, and the deeper it got, the harder it got. Every time he attempted to bring up a shovel of mud, the water rinsed it off the shovel as he moved it through the water to the bucket. When it got deeper he had to dive down to dig it out. The water was so cold he could only work about two hours a day. It took over two weeks to dig the last five feet. Maude was a happy woman when they finally finished the well. Walter recalled being very glad too, that job was finally over.

They named their first child, a son, Timothy. He arrived in 1938 and that was when it all started. Maude wanted a bedroom now that there were three of them, they needed more room. It took Walter four months to cut the trees and build an addition onto the small log cabin. Two years later Anna was born and Maude wanted a loft in the main cabin for the children to use for sleeping. That took him another three months to build.

Around the time he finished building the loft was when he really got into tree farming. Cutting a tree with a bucksaw was hard work, it frequently took a whole day to cut down a tree by himself. Sometimes it would take two days to trim the branches off the fallen tree with a handsaw or ax. Once he got the tree trimmed he cut it up into thirty-foot sections, he hooked up the team of four or six horses and hauled it out to the road. He worked out a deal with Bud Wilson to pick up the logs and haul them to the sawmill five miles away. Bud had a new truck with a tree hauling trailer rig. They both made a tripod type system with a block and tackle to load the logs onto the trailer. After that Bud came by about every three or four weeks to pick up whatever logs Walter had dragged up to the road to go to the mill. Sometimes he'd be back every day for a week or more until he'd hauled away all the logs. Other times it would be just one load of logs, it all depended on how industrious Walter had been during that time. More frequently, it depended on how many jobs Maude had thought up for him to do.

In 1940, every able-bodied young man was going into the Army or Navy to go to war. Walter had a family with two kids to support. More importantly, Walter was supplying the wood to support the war effort. He was deemed exempt from service because the spruce trees he was sending to the mill were essential for building the big bomber airplanes that Boeing was producing. Many of the men in the plant had gone to war so women, like "Rosy the Riveter," came in to replace them. However, there were no women, at the time, out in the woods cutting the trees that were needed to build the airplanes. His services as a logger were critical to the war effort. That was when Walter really started making the money, the government would take every spruce tree he could get to the mill.

About that time someone invented a hand held chain saw that could be used by one person. Up until then the chain saws were not very efficient. They were big, heavy and required two persons to operate. Walter wasted no time getting the new one. It was outrageously expensive, but after using it for two weeks he figured it had already paid for itself. He could cut down and trim four to six trees per day, depending on the size of the tree. He figured his productivity increased by about five hundred percent and best of all, it was much easier on him.

Walter had seen many changes in his lifetime; indoor plumbing, electricity, television, even the Internet, which he knew nothing about. He had to admit, the television was nice to have. In fact, he'd become accustomed to all the new features in the house. In spite of all the work and money it had taken, he decided he didn't want to do without any of the conveniences these days. He wasn't about to dig another well though. His butt was still cold from digging his well over sixty years ago.

In 1955, he bought a track driven tractor type vehicle, similar to a caterpillar or bulldozer, with a blade on the front. He could doze a road with it and then use it to pull out much bigger logs than the horse team could manage.

The invention of the chain saw and the dozer changed Walter's life. Before, he had worked hard every day just to make a meager living. Now he could cut down, trim and haul about four trees up to the road to be picked up by Bud Wilson every day. His bank account began to grow at a rate he and Maude could not believe. By 1966, they had over a million dollars in the bank. He had every type of machinery there was available to make his logging job easier.

When Walter was fifty-one years old he and Maude could've retired easily. Sold the farm and moved to Hawaii and lived in the lap of luxury for the rest of their lives. They took a trip to Hawaii on an airplane or cruise ship every year for two to three weeks. They talked about moving there, but they just couldn't do it, they loved the land too much and they'd worked too hard to make it what it was. The three weeks a year away from their tree farm was just enough to rejuvenate them. They always went in January, when the weather in the northwest was the worst. It was just the break they needed to come back, ready for more hard work. They took the trip every year right up to the year Maude died. After her death, he never went again, it just wasn't the same.

Walter stood up slowly, his arthritis made it hard to get up after picking weeds. He looked around and admired the garden and the fence around it. He built a twelve-foot high fence around the garden out of chicken wire, using small cedar trees he cut from his land to hold it all up. They needed the fence to keep the deer out of the garden. They could jump an eight-foot fence, so it had to be high enough to keep them out. Before he built the fence, about sixty years ago, the deer had eaten everything in the garden.

The garden didn't require much watering in the northwest, there was plenty of rain. Even in the midsummer it usually rained twice a week. August was the only month the garden needed to be watered, it was hot and dry then. Sun was the biggest deterrent to a garden in the northwest, there wasn't enough sun till August. Things grew slowly without the sun, but there always seemed to be enough for them to eat. Especially now that he was by himself.

Walter walked out of the garden and hitched the gate behind him. He looked around as he headed for his favorite stump. Some of the trees were getting blossoms, cherries and pears. All the trees had their new season of leaves popping out in various stages of early spring leafing. Looked like it'd be another good year for the fruit trees.

He sat down on the stump and lit a cigar. It was his only vice, he loved a good cigar. He looked at the old log cabin and admired his work. He'd done a fine job building it, but he sure wouldn't want to build it again today. At eighty-five years old he had a lot more money than energy. Back when he built the cabin he had plenty of energy, lots of trees and ambition, but no money. Today he didn't have much energy, but thanks to the trees he had lots of money, over four million dollars in the bank. Thanks to his land management there was three or four times as much in trees still standing on his property. He loved to plant new trees and watch them grow.

It was unfortunate their children didn't have the same love for the land as he and Maude. He hadn't seen either of them since Maude died over ten years ago. Timothy had joined the Army when he was eighteen. He said working the farm wasn't his kind of job and he wanted to go out to see the world. He stayed in the Army and retired in 1986. His last duty assignment was in North Carolina and he stayed there afterward. The grandchildren were all grown up and they had stayed in the area too. Anna got married right after high school and her husband was transferred to a new job in Portland, Oregon the next year, where they still lived. She called him every month or so to say "Hi" and tell him what they and the kids were doing, but she didn't have time to get up there to see him. Perhaps it was just as well, Walter didn't care much for her husband.

Walter blew out a big blue cloud of smoke, he was lost in his memories. He'd been very lonely for about two years after Maude died. Every once in a while he was deeply affected by her death, much like today. He loved the land and the solitude, but Maude's death was hard on him. They'd just celebrated their fifty-fifth wedding anniversary and had joked for weeks about her stomach swelling. At first they thought she was just gaining weight, later they joked about her being pregnant. When her stomach continued to swell they got concerned and finally decided to go see a doctor.

Walter hadn't been to a doctor in his life. In 1971 Maude was sick with pneumonia and spent three days in the hospital. That was the first time she had seen a doctor. They were both relieved when she came home, but this time it was different, after some tests the doctor said she had a malignant tumor growing in her stomach, and it was a fast growing one. They operated on her the next day to remove the tumor. After the operation the doctor came into the waiting room to talk with Walter. He said that when they opened her stomach her entire insides were a gelatinous mass. He'd never seen anything like it before, he couldn't tell one organ from another. He removed the tumor and closed her up. The prognosis was that it was unlikely she'd live more than a few days. She never regained consciousness after the operation and passed away that night with Walter at her side.

Walter wandered around the property, aimless for months after Maude died. It all happened so fast, and for a long time there was just no purpose to anything anymore. Maude was his only friend and now he was alone.

It was early in the afternoon as Walter finished his cigar. He decided to walk up one of the dirt roads he used to remove the timber and re-plant the trees growing in the roadbed. He hadn't done it for a long time and the seedling trees were beginning to get too big. He got the shovel out of the barn and headed up the road. The horses had been gone for over twenty years, but the barn still served a useful purpose. Now it housed his car and tools. He took the road that headed toward Cross Point and began tenderly digging up the small trees that had planted themselves by nature's means. He then carried them to a good spot in the forest and re-planted them. Instead of simply cutting them down or bulldozing the road, he re-planted each and every tree because he hated to see a tree go to waste. There were logging roads all over the two hundred acres, so it was a job keeping them clear. His property spanned along the border of Newtown on one side and all the way up to the National Forest on the other side, near Cross Point. A lot of property for one eighty-five year old man to keep up, but it gave him something to do.

As Walter worked he realized there weren't any deer around lately and that was strange. In all the years he'd lived there he saw deer almost every day until recently. He knew his land, he knew where they were almost all the time. He could go out and shoot a deer almost any day of the year and it rarely took him more than thirty minutes to find one. For years it had been the reality of life, subsistence. Now, he didn't remember seeing one for weeks and he didn't get it. The forest was quiet, there didn't seem to be many birds around either. Maybe it was his hearing, it wasn't as good as it used to be, he realized the television was turned up almost all the way one night recently. Usually he would see birds flying around in the forest though today there were none to be seen or heard. Maybe it was the Newtown City development that scared everything away. The little town had turned into a big city in the past five years.

Perhaps it wasn't important anymore, he hadn't killed a deer since Maude died. It was much easier to go to the grocery store, there was a big selection of meat and he didn't have to clean and package it. He could certainly afford to buy whatever he wanted or needed and at eighty-five, he didn't feel like working that hard. Just making a meal was more work than Walter wanted.

After three hours of transplanting the trees he figured it would be getting dark before long and he had better quit and head back to the log cabin. He would do this one last tree in the middle of the roadbed. It was a good-sized cedar, about three feet tall, and the roots were well imbedded. He didn't want to kill the tree by cutting off the roots so he got down on his knees and gently pulled at the roots, one at a time.

The two juvenile cougars that recently left Cross Point walked slowly through the woods. They put each paw down with care, to avoid making any noise as they hunted for prey. They'd been wandering around looking for food for days, without any success. The two of them would need to find food soon or face starvation.

They were still in winter fur, their coats were thick with heavy three-inch long fur. This made the cougars look much larger and two cougars traveling together presented an ominous sight. Although they were still considered juveniles, they weighed close to a hundred pounds each.

They were crossing Walter Johnson's property in the northwest sector of the tree farm, not far from Cross Point.   With each step they looked around, moving slowly, looking for deer or any other animal.   They walked out of the woods onto the old logging road, looking both ways slowly, to avoid being spotted by any potential prey.   To the north they saw Walter, walking slowly up the road.   Because they had already eaten a human, this man was potential prey.   Walter was a little unsteady on his feet because of his age and the fact that he had been working all day and was getting tired.   Slowly, careful not to make a sound they headed toward Walter.   As they watched, Walter got down on his knees to dig out the tree, it was the sign the cougars were waiting for.   The male pinned his ears back and like a bolt of lightning took a running leap twenty feet onto Walter's back.   The cougar took the top of Walter's head in its massive jaws as the female moved in closer, but didn't join in on the attack.

Walter felt excruciating pain and knew he was being attacked by something.   He twisted around and thrust the shovel handle into his assailant with all his might.   The cougar didn't yet have a good grip on him and was thrown clear.

Walter took the shovel in both hands and hit the cougar in the side for all he was worth, but it came back quickly with a hiss and a fast swipe with its huge paw, knocking the shovel out of Walter's hands.   That was when he saw the second cougar off to his right side.   He backed up looking for something to use for defense, and raised his arms, waving them around, yelling at the big cats.   As fate would have it, Walter stumbled and fell backward over an old log.   The cougars were on top of him in a flash.   The male clamped his massive jaws on

Walter's throat and his eyes popped out in stark terror.
As Walter struggled to free himself the cougar began
twisting and pulling. Walter's throat was sealed shut so
he couldn't scream. He tried to grab the cougar by the
head, but in seconds the cougar ripped his throat out.

Within hours the cougars had consumed a large part
of Walter and the cats fell asleep. The next morning
when they awoke they began eating again. They licked
the bones of the skeleton all day for the calcium, minerals
and other essential nutrients that animals need. After the
cats departed the area the other animals of the forest; deer,
elk, raccoons, squirrels, possum, badgers, rats, mice and
coyotes would all gnaw on the skeleton for the minerals.
As time went on smaller pieces would be pulled or broken
away and taken off to be consumed somewhere else.
Under these circumstances the skeletal remains could be
spread over a square mile of area within a few months.
Eventually there would be nothing left in the immediate
area.

Walter Johnson had lived on his property for over
sixty-five years. If his remains weren't found in the next
few weeks he would disappear from the face of the earth
without leaving a single trace of his demise. No one
would miss him, no one would even know he was gone
for a long time.

The next day the two cougars started off through the
forest to the south. They wandered around, looking for
food, just as their mother had taught them. Around noon
they came out of the forest into a clearing and saw
Walter's cabin. Normally cougars stay away from people
and houses, but they smelled Walter's scent in the air.
Since they had now eaten two humans, their instinct about
staying away from humans was changed. Humans were
now food and they followed the scent to the cabin.

They walked slowly around the cabin, following the strong human scent, looking for any sign of prey. A cougar's sense of smell is much more highly developed than a human's, but not nearly as good as that of a canine species. The male got up on his hind legs next to a window at the side of the cabin, but he didn't see anything inside. He put his claws into the window casing and pulled down to sharpen his claws, leaving eight deep claw marks in the window casing.

They moved around to the front of the cabin and sniffed at the front door. The male put a paw on the door and pushed. The old door had a latch instead of a doorknob and it was over fifty years old, it swung open. Carefully, he put his head inside and looked around. The scent of Walter was stronger inside and it smelled like food. They both went inside and cautiously walked around the entire cabin. The female went to the counter top and found dirty dishes in the sink. The male defecated on the kitchen floor, leaving a pile of scat. After the female licked all the dishes in the sink clean she urinated in the corner of the kitchen, leaving the telltale cat odor. They went outside and found a big tree next to the barn and both jumped up into the tree and went to sleep. Cougars, like house cats, can sleep eighteen to twenty hours a day.

Cougars are solitary creatures and avoid other cougars, except when kittens are still with the mother learning how to hunt, and during mating. The male woke up in the middle of the night, climbed down the tree and headed northeast toward the housing area of Newtown. When the female awoke she found she was alone. She spent the day wandering around the cleared area near the house and barn. The next day she left and headed south toward the Newtown City maintenance yard.

Photo by Lee Dygert

4

Buck Logan was in the kitchen getting breakfast ready and watching CNBC for the latest stock market update. His favorite software company was up 4 points, looks like a fine day for Internet trading. It was six o'clock a.m., his computer was up and running, he was on the net and he had already checked the individual stock news, half hour till the market opened. But, first things first, he had to get the family off to their daily routine. Buck truly enjoyed retirement, even if he was only forty-five. He'd spent so many years at sea and flying airplanes all over the world that it was nice to be able to spend time with his family, before the children grew up and moved out on their own.

Eric came in and asked, "What's for breakfast?" At sixteen he was full of energy and knew everything that there was to know about life. He quickly changed the television channel to cartoons.

"What sounds good today? I have pancakes or waffles ready to go or if you want I can make you eggs."

"I'll have a waffle," answers Eric as Rob sits down to his plate full of pancakes. Rob, the pancake king, has had three pancakes for breakfast everyday for most of his 14 years. Makes it easy to cook for him, but Buck worries about the sugar fix to get him going in the morning. Maybe it's no worse than the three cups of coffee it takes him to get going. Wendy, 12, is easy to please, she'll eat almost anything Buck puts out.

The phone rings and Eric picks it up. "Hello," after a short pause he says, "Cool. How big was it? Where did you get it? Cool, see you at school."

Buck asks, "What's that all about?"

"It was Jeremiah, he got a deer yesterday up at Table Mountain. It was a three point and weighed about 120 pounds, dressed out."

"Yesterday was a school day. What was he doing out hunting when he should've been in school?"

"Are you kidding? Going hunting on a weekend is like suicide. There're so many people out there hunting on a weekend it's like going hunting at the mall. Hardly any of them are experienced hunters, and they don't know what they're doing. They shoot at anything that moves and then try to figure out what it was after the dust settles. Jeremiah was out hunting last year and somebody shot a tree right next to him. Scared the crap out of him."

"OK, we get the point, but that kind of language is not appropriate for a sixteen year old, or at the table either, for that matter."

He was right though. Many of the people who went hunting today live in the city and grew up in the city.

They know very little about being in the woods, guns or
hunting, but it's a hot topic at work in the northwest
during deer season. Many of the city socialites want to
get in on the action, makes great cocktail party
conversation. There are simply too many inexperienced
people hunting. To top it off, the deer hunting season has
been systematically reduced over the years, causing the
season to be only a few days long at a time.
Consequently, every hunter is out in the woods, using the
same space to hunt, at the same time. Too many people in
too small of a space makes for a dangerous situation and
it increases the likelihood of a hunter getting shot.

"I thought deer hunting season was in the fall."

"It is, but they started a special two day deer hunting
season in March three years ago to thin out the deer
population. You can only take one buck and it has to
have at least two antler points on a side. The deer
population started expanding in 1990 and by 1996 there
were so many deer that the wildlife management people
were afraid the cougar and bear population would explode
too. Deer were everywhere, even in the crowded cities,
interfering with the traffic and causing accidents. So in
1997 they started the special hunt. This year you can only
hunt at Table Mountain. I guess they thinned out the deer
population in the other places."

"That's quite a lot of specific information. Where'd
you learn all that?"

"Jeremiah told me. They talked all about it when he
took the hunter safety course. This will probably be the
last year for a late season hunt. I want to go hunting, and
you keep saying you'll take me. When are we going?"

"I'm going to go hunting today at Safeway. Would
you like steaks or a roast?"

Laughing, Eric says, "Sure Dad, sounds real
exciting."

Things were a lot different when Buck was sixteen years old. Back then he and his father went hunting frequently. Grandma and grandpa lived out in the country. They would visit them on weekends and go hunting in the early morning or evening, practically in their backyard. They usually brought home at least one cottontail rabbit or a quail. They'd skin it, clean it, give it to grandma and she'd put it in the frying pan for dinner. It all seemed pretty normal back then. During deer season they always got a deer, sometimes two. It was common to have a deer hanging on the back porch, curing before they cut it up, wrapped it and put it in the freezer. They had venison all year round when he was a kid. Today it didn't make as much sense. There were too many people, not enough wild country and fewer and fewer wild animals, or so it seemed.

However, in their new neighborhood it was common to see deer in their yard at almost anytime of the day all year. They just walked around through yards and helped themselves to whatever looked good. The neighbors worked long and hard to manicure their yards and spent large amounts of money for plants and shrubs to make the yard look nice. People constantly complained that the deer destroyed their garden. Deer love roses and almost everything that grows in the vegetable garden, especially tomatoes. Everyone had a special remedy or concoction to spray on the plants, especially on the roses. The most effective sprays were primarily raw eggs and red pepper sauce. In the end though, they liked the deer around. Whenever anyone suggesting shooting a few of them, the people were adamant about not harming them, no matter how pesky they were.

"I took you out target shooting just last month."

"No, you and grandpa used to go deer hunting every year. I mean real hunting, like hiking in the woods and stalking the prey. I want to get a deer too."

"Well, I'll think about it, but I think Jeremiah is right about there being too many inexperienced people out there shooting at anything that moves. Hunting season is only four days long for the whole year now. When I was a kid deer season was about three months long. Now everyone is out there in a relatively small space at the same time. Safeway seems like a much more reasonable choice nowadays." There's the macho thing, of course, and the rite of passage etc., but somehow it doesn't all seem as important in the world today as it did thirty years ago.

Buck had been in both the Army and the Navy. He'd been drafted into the Army while he was a sophomore in college. It was during the Vietnam War when virtually every male between eighteen and twenty-four was drafted, if he was not in college. Unfortunately, Buck was working sixty hours a week while attending college. To make matters worse, he was not sure why he was going to college in the first place. Consequently, his grades had suffered badly. He was drafted into the U.S. Army, in spite of being in college, along with thousands of other young men his age. After two years in the Army it was clearly obvious why his parents had told him all his life that a college education was really important. He made a promise to himself that he would get that college degree.

After being discharged from the Army he decided to visit his grandparents for a few days and go hunting. They lived on the eastern side of the Cascade Mountain range and it was a two-hour trip to their house. He'd always enjoyed hunting with his father when he was a teen, but his Dad was working a big logging job at the time.   He was putting in sixty-hour workweeks and couldn't afford to take the time off. Aside from the work schedule, he was getting older and was just too worn-out to go out hiking the hills all day.

Buck decided to go hunting alone. On the trip to grandma and grandpa's he reminisced of times long ago when he and his dad hunted the hills. It'd be a nice few days to relax and unwind. Grandma and grandpa were glad to see him again, and after the greetings and some lunch, Buck went out to the garage to clean grandpa's old 410 shotgun. It only held a single shell and was so old that it could only use the shorter two and a half inch 410 shell. It was nothing fancy, but he had shot many rabbits with the old gun and he liked hunting with it. Grandpa, who was eighty-eight, had bought the shotgun, used, over fifty years ago and he and his father used it for many years before him.

Buck remembered the incident like it was yesterday. It was a beautiful spring morning, the air was crisp, cool and dry, with the sharp smell of wild sagebrush and rosemary in the air.   Every time he smelled sage he remembered those days back when he was a teen hunting with his Dad. He hiked for about an hour from the house to the base of the mountains. The old oak tree was still standing in the middle of the wheat field. It had been dead for many years and was a favorite place for crows and birds of prey to sit up high above the fields and look for prey.   As he was walking along the base of the mountains at the edge of the wheat field, a movement caught his eye.   He looked around and saw a rabbit running through the sagebrush about a hundred yards away. He quickly swung around and fired the old 410 shotgun from the hip, just like in the movies. The rabbit flew back and began to squeal. Buck climbed up to the rabbit as it continued squealing and kicking, he put the heel of his Army boot on the rabbit's head and put an end to its pain. After the crunch of the skull cracking he took the dead rabbit by the hind legs, as he had done so many times before, but this time it was different. It wasn't a full-grown rabbit, and in spite of being a nuisance to the crops, he was sorry that he had killed it. When he stood up, he looked up the hill. Less than twenty feet away was a full-grown cougar, standing there looking right at him. The squealing rabbit probably drew its attention.

He'd never seen a cougar in the wild before, much less up this close. His grandfather had told him there were cougars in the hills, but they're very elusive and rarely seen. They usually sleep in the day and hunt in the early evening and early morning. They go out of their way to avoid people. Only a very hungry cougar will go near people, grandpa had said. They're very strong animals that can kill a full-grown deer and then drag it off to its den or wherever it wants to eat it.

Buck looked the cougar in the eye, knowing it meant business, that was clear. He dropped the rabbit in front of him and slowly walked backward. The cougar took three steps forward. It finally dawned on Buck to raise his shotgun and this seemed to stop the cougar. As he continued backing up he realized his single shot shotgun was not loaded, after he shot the rabbit he hadn't reloaded. He took a shell out of his pocket and reloaded the shotgun, as the cougar snatched the rabbit and headed off up the hill.

Buck was a strong believer in fate. Some of the things that occur in real life are like signs. This hunting trip seemed like a sign to Buck. One, hunting by yourself may not be a good idea, even in an area that had always been a safe place to hunt. Two, there may not be the same reasons to hunt as there once was.

Grandma was disappointed when Buck returned without a rabbit to put in the frying pan for dinner. She

searched around in the freezer until she found them
something to eat. While they ate dinner Buck told them
what had happened. Grandpa said he'd never heard of
anybody being that close to a cougar without being eaten.
"Maybe the rabbit you gave it saved your life?"

He stayed with them for two days and helped grandpa
around the farm, as he'd done so many times before when
he was growing up. They bailed hay and then Buck
picked up the bales and put them on the flatbed trailer
while grandpa drove the tractor. He remembered doing
the same job one summer when he was about sixteen and
it was one hundred ten degrees. Hay chafe stuck to his
sweaty upper body and went into his boots, itching like
crazy. It was the hardest work he could ever remember
doing in his whole life. He learned a lot from grandpa
though, and it was a good time to think and reflect on
where he'd been and where he wanted to go.

That was about twenty years ago and it was the last
time that Buck had gone hunting.

"Oh, I almost forgot. You haven't had the hunter safety
course yet. You can't get a hunting license in
Washington State until you've completed the state
sponsored course, unless you are twenty-six or older."

"Dad, you've taught me a lot more about hunter
safety than they'd ever be able to teach me."

"That may be, but you've got to have the certificate
from the state sponsored course before you can get a
license," Buck responded, liking the pride in Eric's voice.
"I think it's a good idea. Hunter safety is very important,
and too much is a lot better than too little. When I was in
the Navy I had weapons safety training at least once every
year. You know, you could've taken the course last
spring."

"The course was being given during spring break from school. That's family snowboarding week, that week is sacrosanct. There's no way I would give up that week."

Buck and Marie had taken the kids skiing every spring break for the last ten years. It was a ridiculously expensive sport. Still, it was a family togetherness time. 'The family that plays together stays together.' Hopefully, skiing together as a family would last a lifetime. Buck figured skiing or snowboarding was one of the best natural highs that you can get, legally.

They started teaching each of the kids downhill skiing when they were two, at that age they learn fast. Eric and Rob quickly became expert skiers. Wendy had a good time when she was younger, but she got cold easily after a run or two. She spent a big part of her day in the lodge, trying to stay warm and drinking hot chocolate. The boys only went into the lodge for lunch. Any more time in the lodge was considered wasted hill time. As soon as they got off the lift they'd point their skis downhill, go straight to the bottom and get right back on the chair lift as quickly as possible. No downhill time wasted with them. They'd often compete with each other on runs downhill to see who could get to the bottom the fastest. Occasionally, one of them would start a stopwatch at the top of the hill and time the decent. This added a fun new twist to the excitement.

In 1995, snowboarding was just beginning to become popular. It was new and a big thing with the kids, so Eric and Rob decided to give it a try. They both learned to snowboard in one day. They were both very good skiers, but they never got on skis again after that. Snowboarding was the latest thing and a hot topic at school. Seemed like all the kids who went up the mountain in the winter were doing it.

"Well, it's like everything else in life, you have to set priorities. In this case, the snowboarding and the family time together are more important to you than the hunter safety course. There are only so many hours in the day, and you can only do so much. You have to set goals and make your own decisions. By the way, when is the next hunter safety course?"

"The next course isn't until late September. They only give the course twice a year, September and April, during spring break. The September course is during the bowling league."

"Once again, it's all a matter of priorities. Have you signed up for the September one yet?"

"No."

"It's up to you to make the choice and sign yourself up, if that's what you want to do. Just remember you can't get a license without the certificate. The choice is yours."

Buck's wife Marie slowly walked into the kitchen. She was still sleepy and managed to mumble, "Good morning honey."

Cheerfully Buck announced, "Your breakfast is ready, two eggs over easy, two slices of bacon, and a piece of toast. Just the way you like."

It was her favorite breakfast meal and Buck usually fixed it twice a week. Once during the workweek and then again on Sunday, serving it to her in bed with the Sunday paper, something she really enjoyed. All of a sudden she was no longer sleepy and very hungry, as she smelled the coffee and the bacon.

"You're going to turn me into a blimp," she lovingly said as she gave him a quick kiss.

"I'll love you anyway," returning her good morning kiss.

At forty, she looked great and had more energy than most women of twenty-five. They played tennis twice a week, northwest weather permitting, of course. When it was too wet, mostly in the winter, they played racquetball. The racquetball court was indoors at the local school gymnasium. Playing racquetball was dryer and warmer in the winter and was a more strenuous workout than tennis. Too bad there weren't any indoor tennis courts, they'd played tennis for more than twenty years and preferred it to racquetball.

"Well, you know what they say, 'Breakfast is the most important meal of the day'," as he put it on the table.

Marie had a job that she loved as a computer expert for a big software company. She worked with some very talented people and enjoyed the interaction with her co-workers, the variety of personalities provided an intellectually stimulating work environment for her.

"Boys, you'd better get moving or you're going to be late for school. Wendy, you need to get out to the bus stop before its too late. It'll be here in less than five minutes," he barked, "let's go, move it!"

"OK Dad," they all quickly said, adding a hasty, "thanks for the breakfast," they each gave Buck and Marie a hug and were off on their way to school.

Marie thoughtfully said, "You do well as Mr. Mom, but now that you're finished building the house don't you want to get a regular job?"

Buck spent about three years building their house in a nice, new developing area outside the rat race of the big city life. It was hard work and a real challenge, especially since he'd never built a house before. He contracted out the electrical, plumbing, and some of the finishing work. The family helped stuff the insulation, hang the sheet rock and do the mud work on weekends. Building a house was a family tradition, his father and mother built a house a few years after they got married. His grandfather built a house after he retired at the young age of 65. It took Buck about three years to build their new house, but when it was finally finished the whole family was ecstatic. They'd been living in a cramped apartment during the construction. Now each of the children had their own bedroom, and there were three bathrooms, instead of the one and a half that the apartment had. It also had a full basement with a fireplace and a big game room for the children and all their friends to spend countless fun evenings playing video games and watching movies together. The new house seemed immense compared to the little apartment. More importantly, it was all theirs and they now had a permanent place to call home.

It turned out to be a good move for them. Their new neighborhood was really nice, with mountains all around and a natural area surrounding the development. There were trails and watershed areas throughout the community. It was like living in the country, but actually only thirty miles from the big city. The schools were very good and the teachers were great. Most of all, Buck and Marie felt that the children were safe, both in the community and at the school they attended. It was one of the many reasons they'd chosen to live in Newtown.

"What? Me get a job?" Buck feigned shock. "Jobs are for people who don't know how to ski or fish. After flying airplanes in the Navy for twenty years, anything that I could do around here would be anticlimactic. Most of the people around here are working sixty hours a week for forty hours pay. Been there, done that, and I'll never do it again. Besides I don't have time for another job. Between my Navy retirement check, your job, what I make trading stocks, teaching survival at the university and my magazine articles, we don't really need more money. I like not having an eight to five job, I don't think I could ever go back to having a regular daily schedule. I don't think I could stand it. Since it isn't a money issue, I'd rather spend my time with you and the kids."

"You like being around people and feeling that you are needed at work. I don't have any psychological need to be employed any more. Twenty years in the Navy working seventy hours a week or more was enough for me. I like being Mr. Mom. I hardly ever saw the kids when they were little. Now I'm with them every day. I make an adequate amount trading stocks, teaching a little, and writing. It's more than I could make at any regular job around here. Many employers today are stealing from their employees by forcing them to work overtime without paying them for it and that includes salaried employees. It's legal, so they get away with it, but it's wrong. I can do most of my work almost anywhere and if I take off six months, it won't make a difference. I have time to watch the kids at their practice and games. If the kids are out of school and they want to go fishing or play a game of golf, we just do it. By the way, Rob has a soccer game this afternoon after school at four. Will you be able to make it?"

"Wouldn't miss it for the world."

She finished off her breakfast and grabbed another cup of coffee for the road, giving him a kiss on the way out.

"Good-bye Honey, love you, see you later at the game."

"Love you too. Have a fun day."

After the kids and Marie were out the door, Buck quickly found the channel changer and put the TV back on CNBC, the best business news you could get. Just as he found it a local news flash came on, there was a cougar in the Newtown City maintenance yard.

Sally Everheart, Buck's next-door neighbor, was watching the cartoons with her daughter, Sally May, when the news flash came on her television. She quickly changed to the local news station and was intently watching the broadcast with growing alarm, but Sally May had a fit when the cartoons went off. Sally changed the channel back to the cartoons and went into the den to watch the TV there.

A cougar was found in the Newtown City maintenance yard this morning when two employees arrived for work. They were shocked when they drove into the yard to find a cougar eating a raccoon. It had probably just killed it minutes before their arrival. They stayed in their car and watched for about ten minutes before they realized one of them had a cell phone.

The worker dialed 9-1-1 and almost incoherently told of the cougar in the maintenance yard. The operator could barely make out what he was saying because he was speaking so fast. He was probably scared. There was a cougar, right there where he worked all day. The sheriff was quickly dispatched to the scene.

When the sheriff arrived, with lights flashing, it spooked the cougar and it jumped over the back fence and disappeared into the woods. The sheriff grabbed his shotgun off the dashboard of the car and ran to the fence, but it was too late. He couldn't see the cougar anywhere.

One of the two workers asked, "Aren't you going after it?"

Sheriff Tate cried, "Are you nuts? There's no way I'm going out there alone."

The sheriff had twenty-nine years experience in law enforcement. He had worked as a policeman in the big city for ten years before being hired to be the sheriff of

Newtown nineteen years ago. He was eligible to retire anytime, but if he stayed until he had thirty years in law enforcement his retirement check would be substantially higher. He planned to retire to sunny Florida next year. The sheriff knew plenty of law enforcement officers who were killed in the line of duty the day before they were to retire. He didn't intend to get killed before he retired. He worked too hard for that Florida retirement. He planned to lie on the beach, soaking up the rays, drinking a pina colada and smoking a big fat Cuban cigar every day.

Nineteen years ago Newtown was a small, quiet town of 500 residents. It was a great job in those first few years. He welcomed the quiet, laid back attitude of the community after ten years in the high-crime city and all of it's problems. Things had changed greatly for Newtown, especially in the last few years. A big developer came in and subdivided an old farm. There were now two thousand new homes where the old farm had been. Now it was busy and congested, with crime on the rise. He'd hired eight new deputies over the years. The personality of the community had changed too, the new people in town were not as friendly. They were all too busy and very few knew their neighbors anymore. In the past two years a high percentage of the 9-1-1 calls were domestic abuse calls.

In his first few years in Newtown, domestic disputes were a rarity. They were the least favorite type of call for the sheriff's department because they were dangerous. A deputy never knew what to expect when he or she knocked on the door. The occupant may open the door with guns blazing. It was always an unpleasant call because the occupant was rarely calm or contained when the sheriff arrived.

The local news team heard the radio call to dispatch the sheriff to the maintenance yard. They'd arrived only moments after the sheriff's arrival. It didn't take the news team long to set-up the cameras and equipment necessary for an interview. The local news reporter was now interviewing the sheriff.

The reporter asked, "Is this a common thing, for a cougar to be in the maintenance yard, so close to town?"

"I've been Sheriff here in Newtown for nineteen years and I have never seen a cougar around town. For that matter, I've never seen a cougar outside the zoo before."

The reporter rapidly fired off the questions, "What're you going to do? Are you going after it? Are you going to kill it?"

The sheriff thought for a moment before he answered, "Oh no, I'm not going after it by myself. Besides, I'm sure the cougar is well off into the woods by now, too much commotion for it to hang around here. I'll get some deputies over here and we'll take a look around to make sure it is out of the area.   Guess I'll have to talk to the mayor and come up with a plan. The current policy on this type of thing is that we shouldn't shoot it unless it's an immediate threat. In a case like this, it's usually tranquilized and relocated out in the woods someplace. I'll know more after I discuss the situation with the mayor."

Stunned, Sally could hardly believe her ears. The thought of them shooting this beautiful wild animal was unbelievable and she had to do something. This would fit in great with her talk at the Naturalist Club meeting tonight. This new development would present another opportunity to save the natural beauty of the northwest.

Sally had been very active in environmental issues and protests since she was a student at Forevergreen University. When she was a student at the university she participated in many demonstrations, especially saving the trees of the northwest and the spotted owl cause. She felt these activities had been a very positive influence on her university experience and now there were no more unsightly clear-cut forests. She strongly felt the forest belonged to everyone, it didn't matter to her, or her friends, whether the property was public or privately owned.   The national forests, which had previously provided tree farms, were declared off limits to harvesting. Big tree farm owners were tied to public sentiment because of the politics involved. Owners of small private parcels of land and tree farms vehemently protected their rights to do what they chose with their property, in spite of the tree huggers. Her efforts, at least in part, had virtually stopped logging in the northwest. Now the forests would be there for generations to come.

Logging in the northwest was basically like farming. Crops were planted and then harvested, but there was a big difference, most farmers planted their crops and harvested them in two to four months. Trees took about thirty, or more, years before they could be harvested and then replanted. Pulp trees are used for paper and fiber and they grow faster, but lumber trees like fir, spruce, and hemlock take longer.   Most of the trees in the northwest are the lumber type that take over thirty years to harvest. People didn't like looking at the clear-cut hills for the three years or more it took for the newly replanted trees to get some height and cover the clear cut. Evolution in tree farming had brought hybrids and new types of faster growing trees to the northwest. These trees would be used primarily for the pulp to make paper and cardboard. Most of these hybrid trees were being planted on private land, but it still took time. It took approximately ten to fifteen years for the pulp trees to mature. There seemed to be no short-term solution. Wood for building gradually, and steadily, got more expensive, due to the developing supply and demand situation.

The result was that thousands of people became unemployed almost overnight. There were families that had been loggers for generations whose livelihood completely disappeared. In the big picture, the environmentalists said this seemed insignificant. In the northwest, it was devastating. About twenty percent of the jobs in the northwest were tied, in some way, to logging. If you take twenty percent of the jobs away anywhere, it's a big deal.

After the spotted owl cause successfully stopped all logging in the northwest, Sally and a group of her friends moved on to a new cause, to stop hunters from using dogs to hunt cougars and bears. They claimed this type of hunting was cruel and unusual punishment for the animals. Even when the hunters did not kill the animals, it was harassment to them and made them nervous and irritable. After Sally graduated she continued with the cause. She and her friends spent the next two years picketing in front of the state capitol one day per month. They also spent one day a week at a local mall or grocery store with signs and brochures. They circulated petitions to gain signatures for a new law that would outlaw hunting with dogs.

They researched their plan while still in college and found that only about half of the state voters actually vote. They also discovered that more than half of those voting were women. Her environmentalist group was an equal mix of men and women, but since hunting was a man thing they soon discovered that if they targeted the women shoppers they had better results getting signatures. In the end, once they got the measure on the ballot they only needed 51 percent of the votes to win.

Their end goal was to have all guns made illegal in the state, both handguns and rifles. They figured if the federal government couldn't do it, they'd do it at the state level, by chipping away at hunting slowly, bit by bit.

Once they were successful at banning dog hunting they would start an initiative to stop deer hunting, then birds. Eventually their goal was to make all hunting illegal. When this happened there would be no need for guns and they would start an initiative to make the sale or possession of guns in the state illegal.   They were all convinced they would win, even if it took a lifetime.

It took the group over two years, but in 1996 they finally succeeded in making hunting cougars or bear with dog's illegal.   Still in the early stages of working on a plan to stop deer hunting, they figured this one would take 3-4 years. Regardless of the time involved, they were all confident they would succeed.

Their major issue was that people did not need to hunt anymore. There were grocery stores everywhere and most people could easily buy anything they needed to eat. Hunting had outlived its purpose and now it was time to move into the twenty-first century and stop the barbarian practice of killing wild animals.

Sally finished getting breakfast for her children, Will, seven, and Sally May, five.   It was the usual bowl of highly sweetened cereal, orange juice and toast, heavily laden with cinnamon and sugar.   They were totally consumed watching the morning cartoons on television while they ate their breakfast.

"Oh my god, did you hear the news Doug? There's a cougar in the Newtown City maintenance yard and they want to kill it. I can hardly wait for the Naturalist Club meeting tonight," she said as her husband, Doug, walked into the kitchen.

Doug poured himself some coffee in a large car travel mug for those on the go. It was a long drive to his office and he needed something to get him going on the way. He did well as an insurance salesman but the hours were very long. Doug was tall, handsome, played football in high school and college and he was a workaholic. Usually he left home around six forty-five and returned home between eight and ten at night. He almost always worked on Saturday and occasionally met clients or did paperwork at home on Sundays.

"I'm giving a presentation at the Naturalist Club meeting tonight. How does this sound?" Sally was ready to read it to Doug. She'd been rehearsing her presentation over and over in her mind for two days, eagerly changing her notes and outline to sound perfect, just as her college speech class professor had taught her. She was eager to hear Doug's opinion now that the day was here and she felt her speech was finally ready. The cougar story would be a great add-on.

"I'd really love to hear it honey, but I'm running late and I have a new client meeting me at the office at eight o'clock. With all the traffic from our new house to the office, I'll barely make it to the office on time to be ready for the meeting."

"Are you sorry we moved out here to Newtown? We didn't think the thirty-mile drive would be a problem. It's almost all freeway, and the schools are so good. It's like being able to live in the country and have all the advantages of the city here at our doorstep," Sally said, disappointed.

"No, I love it here dear," said Doug. "The traffic's really getting more congested with all the new houses going in though. It takes over an hour to get from home to my office, if I'm lucky. That's why I come home so late. It only takes thirty-five minutes if I leave the office after seven o'clock."

"I sure wish you didn't have to work such long hours. We hardly ever see you anymore. You never seem to have time to enjoy our new home."

Doug wished he didn't have to spend so much time driving. Sitting in the car for over two hours every day was such a waste of his time. Time he could be using to pitch a new client or on the phone trying to make a new appointment. The mortgage on the new house was higher than the old mortgage and he wanted to start putting some money into the stock market. It just kept going up and up and he wasn't along for the ride, yet. The house payment, two new car payments, and the outrageous cost of medical health care insurance, plus everything else, there was just not enough money left at the end of the month to invest. Driven to make more money, he wanted to ride the wave of the future and make a killing like everyone else at work. His co-workers were always talking about how much money they made in the market last week. Those Internet and biotech stocks are really hot, they'd say. Most of the Internet stocks were over one hundred dollars a share. He couldn't even pull together enough extra money at the end of the month to buy even one share. His priorities were focused on his career.

"Got to run honey," and he was out the door before anyone could say anything. Not even a kiss good-bye or a word to the kids.

Will and Sally May felt rejected. "We'll listen to your speech Mommy. How come Daddy is always in such a hurry? I wanted to play catch with him yesterday, but he said he was too busy. He said he had to get ready for his meeting today."

"I know honey, Daddy's schedule at work has been hard on all of us. Thanks for the offer to help me Will, but I think I need to have an adult listen to my speech. I need some constructive criticism. Sort of like a teacher, to give me a critique. I haven't given a speech in front of a lot of strangers in a long time."

Sally returned to her thoughts, the meeting tonight will have a reporter from a Seattle newspaper. She needed to sound professional and knowledgeable. She made some notes to talk about the killing of the cougar too.

"Besides, it's time to brush your teeth and get out to the bus stop. I don't want you to miss the bus. Then I'd have to drive you to school, again."

Will was so mesmerized by the cartoon show that he didn't hear a word his mom said. Sally put her hand on his shoulder to break the cartoon trance.

"Get out to the bus stop right now," as she was handing him his lunch money.

Will reluctantly got up and grabbed his backpack. He walked backward, watching the same cartoon show that he had seen at least twenty times before, so he wouldn't miss any of it before he got to the door. Off he went, as the bus was coming down the street.

It was always a mad dash at the last minute, Sally thought, as she watched him get on the bus. She had to drive him to school about once a week because he didn't get out to the bus on time. He frequently slept in too late and was hard to get moving in the morning because he stayed up too late the night before. The excuse he pitched was that he wanted to stay up till Dad got home from work. She wasn't sure if that was the real reason. He pretty much just wanted to stay up and watch television as long as he possibly could.

"OK Sally May, you too, let's get moving. I have to go shopping and then out to lunch today. You are going to the baby-sitter until it's time for her to take you to school for your afternoon kindergarten class."

"I want to go shopping too," said Sally May, pouting.

"Sorry, this is big people shopping and I'm meeting Cheryl, my old college pal from Forevergreen University, for lunch. Hopefully she'll be able to help me with my speech."

Photo by Lee Dygert

5

Buck was finishing up his three-mile jog, slowing to a fast walk for the last block. He was hot and sweating heavily, in spite of the fifty-five degree day. It was a beautiful clear northwest spring day, but still a little cool in the afternoon. The flowers were beginning to bloom and that fresh spring aroma of the evergreens was in the air. Of all the places Buck had lived and traveled he'd never smelled that fresh, spectacular aroma that permeates the northwest in the spring time anywhere else. It was a fantastic fragrance that he had cherished since his childhood.

Frank Wilson was out in his front yard trimming his hedge as Buck walked past. Frank was somewhere between seventy-five and eighty. He lived by himself and seemed to be a rather cantankerous old coot. He probably was lonely, but most likely he had always been crotchety.
"Afternoon Frank. How you doing?"
"I'm not worth a damn. My cat didn't come home last night. She's the only company I have anymore.

She's always there, followed me around the yard all day yesterday. When I finished the yard and went into the house, she was nowhere to be found, and she hasn't come home yet."

"Oh, she'll be back, just be patient. Don't worry, cats are always taking off for a few days. Hey Frank, you missed a spot on the hedge over here," Buck pointed out as he continued walking up the street.

Still complaining, Frank said, "By the way, Buck, how about keeping your kids and their friends out of my yard. They make too much noise."

"I'll be sure to talk to them about it Frank." Seemed like he always had something to complain about.

Buck was in excellent physical condition for forty-five years old. He had been a star swimmer in high school and a team captain on the water polo team. During his years in the Navy, physical fitness was mandatory. All Navy personnel took a physical fitness test every six months. Those who didn't pass the test had compulsory remedial fitness training for one and a half hours, three days per week and they stayed on the program until they could pass the test. Anyone who couldn't pass the test after six months was discharged. The test consisted of sit-ups, push-ups, pull-ups and either a mile and a half run or a 500-meter swim at the base pool. The swim at the pool was a piece of cake for Buck who easily beat everyone else, sometimes lapping other swimmers four or five times in the five hundred yards. He carried these life long exercise habits with him after he retired from the Navy and he tried to exercise daily in some way or another.

As he cooled down from his run he wondered if he'd ever be able to loose any weight. If he were still in the Navy, he would be approaching the top of his weight limit for passing the weight standard. Much of the weight was muscle, which is more dense than fat, consequently it weighs more, but there was some fat beginning to show around the waist.

Six months earlier Buck saw Dr. West, the family doctor, for an annual physical. After all the tests were completed Dr. West announced, "You are in excellent physical condition, fit as a fiddle, for a man your age."

His concern was the expanding waistline. After he finished building the house he got out of the habit of exercising daily and gained about ten pounds. He restarted his exercise program about seven months ago.

He asked Dr. West, "That's nice to hear, but what can I do about this excess around the middle? I diet and exercise, but nothing seems to do any good."

"Are you over forty?" The doctor was also over forty years old and had a bit of a spare tire around the middle himself.

"Yes, you know I am."

"It's hopeless, just do the best you can. After people turn forty the body begins to change, physiologically, and the metabolism slows down. After forty, there's a propensity for people to exercise less. It hits some people around forty years of age, others, who have been more physically active, don't begin to experience the weight gain until after fifty. They don't have the time to exercise, they work too much, there is too much pain after working out or they're just too tired. People also, ironically, tend to eat more. They're more financially stable and they can afford it. It's a bad combination eating more and exercising less."

"My best advice is one plate of dinner, no seconds. No dessert after dinner, no fatty foods, especially ribs, bacon, donuts. Cut down on anything that has sugar in it, like ice cream, and continue on your exercise program.

You should exercise moderately for one to one and a half hours at a time, at least three times per week. The people who seem to have the best luck with keeping their weight in check walk about an hour after breakfast or dinner every day, seven days a week. That's about the best advice I can give you. Good luck."

As Buck walked up his driveway, Sally was out in her front yard picking a bunch of flowers.

"Hi Sally. Your flower bed is really doing great this year."

"Thanks, it's nice to be able to pick some flowers. The daffodils and the tulips are my favorites. Usually the deer come through here every few days and eat everything in sight, especially everything that's starting to blossom. They especially like my roses. Now that I think about it, I haven't seen a deer for weeks and the garden is finally beginning to take hold. "

"You know, I think you are right, I haven't seen a deer lately either. Usually I chase them out of the yard every few days, but when they come in the middle of the night there isn't much that can be done about it. Guess we'll just have to live with them destroying our gardens or else plant something the deer don't like. I hear they won't eat rhododendrons or azaleas. Some of the people in the neighborhood build fences around their gardens, I don't think it does any good. The deer just jump over the fence unless it's more than six feet high. They'll be back."

"It's a small price to pay. I like the deer in the yard, makes our neat neighborhood seem more like the country."

"Yes, it's a nice place to live."

Buck went into the house and showered. He hadn't been out of the shower long when the school bus pulled up in front of the house. As it stopped, the doors swung open and the kids jumped out, running away from the bus in all directions. Rob ran up the driveway and in the door.

"How come you didn't come home with Eric?"

"He stayed after school to do a project in the library and I forgot to take my soccer uniform to school. I need to get to the field quick or the coach won't let me play today."

Grabbing his keys, Buck said, "OK. Get your stuff and let's go."

Sally gathered the flowers, took them into the house and arranged them in a nice blue vase. She decided to put the arrangement on the kitchen table so everyone could enjoy them.

"There," she said to no one but herself, "that really makes the kitchen look cheerful."

She sat down at the computer to put the finishing touches on her speech for the Naturalist Club tonight. She would fight for the cougar's right to survive. She was so excited about her new cause she could hardly contain herself.

Sally was still working on her speech when she heard the school bus pull up across the street in front of her house. As the door opened, the children spilled out in all directions, all yelling, running and playing, happy to be home from school.

Across the street was one of many natural areas throughout the neighborhood. There were lots of old trees and brush in a fairly dense growth area with a few trails that went throughout the woods from one neighborhood to another. Most of the trails were big enough for two bikes to ride side by side. Adjacent to the bus stop was a big, old cedar tree. About fifteen feet above the ground, almost directly above the bus, and nearly invisible, was a cougar lying on a big branch, hidden by the foliage of the tree. Lying in this same tree each afternoon for the last two days, it watched the children as they walked beneath him. He was becoming accustomed to being around humans. Humans were now food to the cougar, but he also understood there is danger around humans, sensing the need to wait for the right opportunity. Everyone was completely oblivious to his presence.

Will and Sally May came in the house running, out of breath, but excited to be home. They were ready for a snack and anxious to tell mom about their day at school. Sally May threw down her backpack and turned on the television to the afternoon cartoons.

"I'm hungry, what do we have to eat?"

Sally set out a plate of cookies and gave them each a cola, no milk for her kids. While she was in college she did research for a term paper in a genetics class. Since she was allergic to milk and allergies are frequently passed on genetically she decided her children wouldn't drink milk. Consequently, they avoided almost all dairy products of any kind.

Sally May was rambling on about what happened to her at school that day, but Sally wasn't listening. She was already back at the computer, deeply involved in her speech. Sally May soon realized that mom was self-absorbed and wasn't listening to her so she took one of Will's cookies and quickly downed it. Will grabbed her hair and started yelling at her. Sally May grabbed her soda and threw it all over Will.

"Stop!" yelled Sally. By then, Sally May and Will were in full battle. They completely ignored Sally.

"I can't deal with this today, both of you go to your rooms, Now!" But they kept fighting, continuing to ignore her.

She got up and took each one by the arm and escorted them to their rooms, closing the door behind them. She went back to her speech while Will continued to scream through his closed door at Sally May.

Buck and Rob got to the game in plenty of time. Rob chose to play on an independent team instead of the high school team. There was too much politics with the school team. On the independent team everyone played at least fifty percent of the time, it is mandated by the sport and a great idea thought Buck. This method eliminated the favorites and the good old boy philosophy that seemed to dominate many school sports today. Ability was not the important thing and Rob had a great time and a lot of fun.

Buck set his lawn chair down next to Jim Boom and Terry Marker, they'd struck up a friendship while watching the kids play soccer. Jim had worked for the same company for twenty-five years. He went to work one day and got a pink slip in the envelope with his check, he was laid off. That was over a year ago. There was a real irony here. It was the ideal situation, sort of, he had a nice retirement check, and at only fifty-one, it was like a dream come true, retire early and have fun. The problem was that he didn't want to retire yet.

Jim spent the last year trying to find employment. He worked at it forty hours a week, just like a job. He couldn't get an interview for anything, whether he was qualified or over qualified, in spite of a college degree and years of experience. It was frustrating to him. He couldn't even get an interview for an entry-level job at the fastest growing hardware store in town. They had a 'help wanted' sign on the front door of the store and the store employees said they were crying for help.

Marie arrived and put her chair down next to Buck, "Hi honey, hi guys," and gave Buck a kiss on the cheek.

"Hi honey, how was your day?"

Jim and Terry both said, "Hi Marie."

"Oh fine, same as usual. Nothing of any particular interest today."

"Game's going good, no score yet though," Buck said as he returned to his conversation with Jim and Terry.

"I don't think things are going to change in time for it to make any difference for people our age. You like to do wood work, and you have a well-equipped shop, find a way to make some money doing something you love." Buck sagely added, "If you can make money doing something you love, you will never work a day in your life."

The game was about half over when one of the parents yelled, "Cougar! Over there! It just went into the woods!"

For an instant everybody froze in place. Then the game officials gathered all the players together and herded them over to the sidelines where all the parents and spectators were standing. The group of people began to speculate. It seemed to Buck like cougar mania, everyone at the game was talking about the cougar sighting at the maintenance yard this morning. He heard people saying that they were going to build a fence around their backyard to keep the cougar out, like a fence would work.

Buck, Terry, and Jim decided to go over to the place where the woman had seen the cougar and check it out. They walked up to the edge of the woods and looked into the foliage, it was too dense to see very far. They walked up and down the edge of the woods about fifty yards, but didn't see anything. They came to a trail so they decided to go into the woods. Buck led the way and they proceeded with caution. He understood enough about cougars to know that it was very unlikely one would attack three full-grown men. After about thirty feet on the trail they heard something moving around in the bushes. They all jumped back, their hearts pounding in their chests, wondering whether to run or stand their ground. Out came a large yellow Labrador retriever, tail wagging, friendly as could be.

Buck let the dog smell his hand and the dog licked it. Taking the dog by the collar he brought it out of the woods to the soccer field for everyone to see. The crowd was obviously relieved and the coaches got the players all re-organized. The referees re-started the game, but it didn't have the usual fervor.

After the game was over Buck and Rob were walking back to the car. While they were walking through the parking lot, they overheard one of the other team member's father yelling at his son because he didn't take the shot at the goal when he had a chance. The father hit his son on the back of his head, angrily telling him that he was a gutless failure.

Continuing with his tirade he said, "You have to get in there and go for the kill, winning is the only thing that matters."

When they were in the car and on the way home Rob sadly asked, "Why are people like that? That man hit his son because he didn't make a goal. Who cares? It's just a game."

"You are absolutely right son, it's just a game. Unfortunately, some people don't see it that way. Some parents try to live their own lives vicariously through their children. They think their children can make up for their own failures in life. If their children become successful, they can ride the wave of success through their children. It's a pitiful situation, but unfortunately, there are always a few people like that in kid's sports."

"Sporting events cause people to get very excited and that's a good thing. When a person attacks someone else, if things don't go their way, that's not acceptable behavior. Can you imagine the effect the incident has on his son? Most likely his son will quit the team soon. I've seen it before. It's highly likely the son will never have anything to do with sports for the rest of his life. Is that the kind of example you want to set for your children?"

"No, he was an idiot."

Sally was really fired up as she worked intently on her speech. The sound of the doorbell ringing startled her and when she got to the door she was surprised to see that it was Irene, the baby-sitter. She was even more surprised to see that it was dark outside.

Sally opened the front door, "Oh no! What time is it?"

"It's six o'clock. Just like you said, 'be here at six'."

"Thanks for being on time Irene, I really appreciate it. I was so wrapped up in writing my speech outline that I lost track of the time." Suddenly, Sally noticed Irene looked a little shook up.

"You look like you saw a ghost. Are you all right?"

"I heard a noise while I was walking over here. It was real eerie."

"Like what kind of noise?"

"I don't know, it was kind of a deep growl. There was something in the bushes next to the path. From the sound of the growl it must have been fairly big. It made my skin crawl and I ran the rest of the way here. It was way scary."

"I'll drive you home tonight when I get back from my meeting. I shouldn't be too late, probably be home around nine o'clock. Doug will be working late and will probably get home later than me, but if he does get home first make sure he either takes you home or have one of your parents pick you up. Either that or wait for me to get back and I'll take you home."

"Great, thanks I'd be grateful for a ride. I don't want to walk home tonight after that scary experience."

Sally was really running late now so she changed her clothes as fast as she could. As she was running out the door she called out to Irene.

"Can you please make dinner for the kids? There's frozen dinners in the freezer, just heat them according to the directions. They usually eat around six thirty." She quickly went into the garage, jumped into the car, slammed the door shut and was on her way downtown.

"Sure, no problem." She seriously doubted Sally heard her.

There were a lot of people milling around talking when Sally arrived, it was about fifteen minutes after the scheduled start time. The meeting finally got started and there was about a hundred people in the audience, certainly a lot more than Sally had expected. Some were college students, some were high tech workers with lots of money, and some were middle aged. Nearly all of them were from the city. The high tech workers had a special interest group that wanted to preserve nature for all eternity. They all felt the forests were disappearing too fast and something had to be done. They wanted to be able to go out on the weekends and go hiking in the undisturbed wilderness, taking a hundred other people along with them for security.

Sally's turn to speak came close to the beginning of the meeting. As she got up and walked to the podium, she realized how nervous she really was, she hadn't been in front of an audience for years, even though she'd rehearsed the speech over and over in her mind all day. She placed her notes on the podium, looked around the room, and saw some familiar faces. In the front row sat the local newspaper reporter. He was all business, with the recorder running, and taking notes frantically. A rather handsome looking young man, she thought. He looked up at her and smiled, easing her tension.

"My name is Sally Everheart. I have been a member of the Naturalist Club for almost eight years."

The nervousness disappeared as she started her speech and she felt good, in fact she was exhilarated by what she was saying.

"I see a few familiar faces and some new ones too. When I was a student at Forevergreen University I was very active in the environmental movement. I helped organize and have participated in many protests at the National Forests to stop the clear cutting of our heritage, our property. I was arrested three times during the protests for trespassing and whatever trumped up reason they could come up with. The taxes we pay support our National Forests. These criminals had been raping our land, our property, for too long. Our efforts produced an endangered species list, the spotted owl being the most famous. Now more and more animals are being added to that list. This will increase the protective nature of our cause and ensure the forests are there for our grandchildren to enjoy as much as we enjoy them today."

"I was also on the committee to stop cougar and bear hunters from using dogs to find their prey. We were finally successful in stopping this barbaric and inhumane practice when the voters approved the new law four years ago."

"I believe I have a new cause for us today that is equally important. I live in the small community of Newtown about thirty miles east of here. It's an older town that's experiencing new development."

"The city officials have been yielding to the complaints of the town's people to get rid of problem animals. They complain the deer, raccoons, and possums eat their gardens or get into their trashcans and spread the trash all over the street. These animals were here first. It's their home and the people have moved into their territory. There is absolutely no reason why we cannot coexist here together. We need to formulate some new laws to protect these animals."

"Some of you may have seen the news today about a cougar being seen in the Newtown City maintenance yard this morning. The city officials are now trying to develop a plan to kill the cougar. This is ridiculous, but it's so typical of government thinking. This is simply an excuse for them to begin killing off all the wild animals around our town."

"We need to band together and present a united front, so we can stop this wholesale slaughter of our wildlife. If we don't, they'll kill off all the animals until they become extinct too. The cougar is such a beautiful animal. This is just the beginning. Once the cougar is killed, the officials will systematically kill off all the animals. We have to stop them now before it is too late. I propose we get a committee together to go to the Newtown City meeting tomorrow night. We need to protest this outrageous assault on our wildlife."

Hearing this last comment got the crowd fired up. "No! They can't do that!" was the overwhelming cry from the audience. The crowd began to complain, "Let nature take care of itself. Don't interfere with nature.

Leave the animals alone. The people are the one's at fault, not the animals."

A committee was formed to represent the club and attend the meeting in Newtown the next night. They'd fight any effort to upset the natural balance of nature. They all agreed, "Let nature be."

Buck's father and mother were over for dinner. Buck's father, Jack, was a logger for forty years. He was a rugged man and still in excellent physical condition for seventy-five years old. Buck's mother, Mary, had been a sixth-grade schoolteacher for over twenty years and she still did volunteer work at the school two days a week. She loved the classroom and helping children learn.

Buck and Marie chose to live in Newtown when he retired from the U. S. Navy. It's only twenty minutes from where he grew up and where his parents still lived. They were getting older and, while his parents had visited them many times over the years when he was in the Navy, his parents didn't like to travel anymore. Travel was too confusing to them, too much hassle, and it made them too tired. They simply liked the comfort of their own home, it was familiar, secure and there's no place like home.

While they were all at the table eating dinner Buck said to the boys, "I talked with Frank this afternoon when I was coming back from my jog. He asked me to have you and your friends stay out of his yard. What were you doing in his yard anyway?"

"We were playing 'ghost in the grave yard' last Saturday night. He came out of his house and yelled at all of us," said Rob.

"You mean Grumpy? That old geezer complains about everything," lamented Eric.

"Well, after all it's his property, and he doesn't have any kids out playing with you guys. He also goes to bed early, about nine o'clock. It's his yard, you need to stay out of it."

"OK," they both said.

Buck looked at his father, "Did you hear about the cougar in the Newtown City maintenance yard this morning?'

"Yes, I saw it on the news this afternoon. Pretty unusual for a cougar to get this close to houses and people."

"It seems like there's been a lot of cougar sightings inside city limits around the state in the past year. You see it on the news about once a month. First time we've had one in Newtown though. We used to hunt a lot when I was a kid, but we never went cougar hunting. Have you ever been cougar hunting?" Buck asked, curious about the animal.

"Yes. "

"Are they hard to hunt?"

"You know how you don't like to talk about your Naval Aviator friends that got killed in plane crashes?"

"Yes."

"Well, it's kind of the same thing. My one cougar hunting experience was a bad one."

Buck's curiosity was strong, but he also realized the similarities in his dad's expression. Buck knew the feeling all too well. Talking about the airplane accidents his Navy friends had been killed in was very difficult for him. You have to be in the right frame of mind to get through it all. Besides, he felt the dinner table wasn't the right place for that kind of conversation.

Sally got home from the meeting at nine fifteen and paid Irene, "I'll take you home. Kids, it's time for you to get to bed."

They both whined, "But Dad's not home yet. We have to stay up until he gets home so we can say goodnight to him."

"I'll have Dad come tuck you in when he gets home. He'll be here any minute now. Go get your teeth brushed and your pajamas on. I'm taking Irene home, I'll be back in five minutes."

They went into the garage and got in the car. She pressed the garage door opener, started the car and backed out, leaving the garage door open. She'd only be gone a few minutes.

The cougar stayed in the same tree across the street from the Everhart's house until dark. He then dropped effortlessly out of the tree and begun wandering around the neighborhood under the cover of darkness. He was walking around the side of Buck's house when the noise of Sally's garage door startled him. After Sally pulled out of the garage the cougar walked slowly over to Sally's and went into the garage. It began searching around the garage, looking for something to eat. As he studied the door, Muffy, their poodle, came into the laundry room and went to the door. She smelled the cougar, felt its presence, and began to bark. The kids were upstairs changing into their pajamas and didn't hear anything. The cougar instinctively knew that dinner was on the other side of that door, how to get to it was the problem.

The cougar put its front paw on the door and pushed, but it didn't give. He ran his claws down the door, leaving four scratch marks about two feet long, but still no success getting at the dog. He heard a car coming down the street and walked over to a corner in the garage, next to some tan colored cardboard boxes, just as the car turned into the driveway and pulled into the garage. As the car door opened the cougar crouched next to the cardboard boxes, he was almost the same color as the boxes. He stayed there very still and watched.

After Doug shut off the engine and car lights, he got out of the car. The garage light was out and the garage was dark. He thought it odd that the garage door had been left open. As he went into the house he pressed the button to close the garage door. He went straight to the bar, poured a glass full of scotch, took a swig, and went to the refrigerator. He put two ice cubes into the glass, went upstairs to his bedroom and set the drink down on the nightstand. Then he went into Will's room.

"Where's Mom?"

"She took Irene, the baby-sitter, home. Irene was afraid to walk home in the dark. Mom said she'd be right back."

Doug tucked in Will and said good night. Then he went to Sally May's bedroom and tucked her in and gave her a kiss and said good night to her. After that he went straight to bed to finish up his glass of scotch while he looked at an insurance contract for a proposal for the next day.

The cougar was trapped in the garage and he didn't like this turn of events one bit. He paced back and forth around the garage. The dog came back to the door and started barking again, agitating the cougar. He went over to the door, and listened to the dog on the other side and let out a deep toned hiss. Muffy jumped back with her tail between her legs and started to yelp, as if she'd been hit. The cougar pawed at the door trying to push it open, leaving more scratch marks on the door.

Doug thought he heard something and wondered what it was. As he listened, it sounded like Muffy was hurt. He got out of bed and went downstairs to find

Muffy in the laundry room, which had the door leading
into the garage.   Muffy sat there yelping with her tail
between her legs and looking at the door, fear in her eyes.
Doug went over to the door and reached for the doorknob.

As Sally drove down the street, she saw that the
garage door was closed.   She could have sworn she'd left
the door open.   It was plenty safe in this neighborhood,
nothing to worry about.   There'd never been a robbery or
any other kind of problem that she heard of.   Reaching
over she took the garage door opener out of the glove
compartment and pressed it as she drove down the street.

Doug opened the door to the garage, just as the
garage door began to open.   The door opening caught him
by surprise.   He looked into the garage, but apparently the
opener light, that was supposed to go on when the door
started up or down, had gone out and the garage was dark.

Sally took her eyes off the road, and the garage, as
she placed the garage door opener back in the glove
compartment.   As she did this, the cougar bolted out of
the garage and disappeared into the darkness.

Doug reached over on the wall and turned on the
other garage light.

Sally pulled into the garage and got out, "Hi honey,
nice of you to meet me at the garage."

"Hi Sally."   He gave her a kiss and pressed the
button to close the door as they walked into the house.
Muffy was sitting in the laundry room and she seemed to
be OK now.   They went upstairs and Doug went back to
bed as Sally tucked in the kids one at a time and gave
each a kiss goodnight.

She went into her bedroom and gave Doug a
meaningful kiss.   "I've missed you.   You work too
much."

Doug put his papers down on the bed.   " Yeah I
know, I'm bushed.   This job is too much work.   It never
seems to end."

The dog was barking downstairs. "I have to let Muffy out and fold the clothes. I'll be right back. Don't go to sleep."

Sally May got out of bed to look out the window and see what was making the dog bark so much. It was light inside and dark outside so she couldn't see more than a few inches through the glass. There were no streetlights in their neighborhood and it was a dark and cloudy night. She stood there staring at the window.

The cougar roamed in the darkness looking at the back of the house. It knew there was food inside, but it didn't know how to get to it. When Sally May came to the window she got his attention and he quickly jumped up onto the garage roof and then onto the roof of the house. Slowly the cougar moved over to the window where Sally May stood, but as he got closer to the window Sally May disappeared.

"Sally May, you get back into bed. It's too late for you to be up."

"But Muffy's barking so much. Why's she barking? She never barks unless something is wrong."

"She just wants to go outside for her evening ritual. Goodnight. Love you," as she gave Sally May a hug and a kiss and moved quietly toward the door.

She went downstairs and let Muffy out the sliding glass door to the backyard. It was ten o'clock, about the same time she usually let Muffy out for her nightly routine.

The cougar put his nose up to the window, it was open about one inch at the bottom. He sniffed at the opening, smelling the inside of Sally May's room. He took his paw and pushed at the window, but it wouldn't move.

The sliding glass door at the back of the house opened and Muffy took off for the tree line in the

backyard, same as she always did every night.   Each
house in the neighborhood was on roughly one acre of
land. Most of the houses had a big front and back lawn,
with lots of trees. None of the yards had fences so the
backyard was open to the natural area. Muffy sniffed
around and caught a new scent, following it for a few
minutes.

The cougar heard the sliding glass door open and saw
Muffy sniffing around. He easily jumped off the roof and
began to stalk Muffy. Sudden Muffy froze in place. She
recognized the scent from earlier in the evening when she
was at the door to the garage in the laundry room.

After Sally let Muffy out, she went to the laundry room
and unloaded the clothes dryer and started folding the
clothes. The nightly routine was familiar to both of them
and took about the same amount of time every night. She
folded clothes while Muffy went out to relieve herself, do
all the sniffing and come back to the glass door.

Sally thought about her meeting that night downtown
and the local town meeting tomorrow night. She kept
going over the events of the day in her head and how it all
would fit into her presentation at the meeting tomorrow.
She began to mentally formulate a speech for tomorrow's
meeting.

Muffy took off for the house like an air-to-air missile.
She hit the door scratching with both front paws, pawing
the door for all she was worth. The scratching was so
intense, her claws began to etch the glass.

Sally put some of the laundry back into the dryer, the heavy towels weren't quite dry yet. The dryer was noisy and she couldn't hear anything else but the dryer running and the towels banging around against the sides. It wouldn't take much longer for them to finish drying, in the mean time she'd fold the rest of the clothes.

Muffy was exhausted. She looked back over her shoulder, there on the patio ten feet behind her, was a big, mean, snarling cougar. It was one hundred pounds of sheer muscle, teeth, claws and appetite. The cougar's ears were pinned back, mouth open, fangs showing, a sign the cougar was about to make an attack. Muffy instinctively knew it was going to attack her so she bolted to the left, but he cut her off. She quickly turned right and was boxed into a corner. Muffy hunched down, cowering and shaking. She was so scared she started to urinate and defecate at the same time. The cougar knew this was easy prey and just walked slowly up to the dog, quickly grabbed the dog behind the head. He turned around with Muffy in his massive jaws and headed for the woods.

Muffy felt the pain of the cougar's teeth on the back of her neck and attempted to free herself. She shook and tried to scratch the cougar with her rear paws, trying to get away. The cougar didn't want to be injured by the dog's claws so he clamped down with his powerful jaws driving the long canine teeth between the vertebrae and breaking its neck. The dog went limp and its head lolled fell off to the right. The dog's body dragged on the ground between the cougar's front legs as he trotted across the lawn and into the woods. As he trotted off toward the woods, Sally opened the sliding glass door.

"Muffy!" It was dark and Sally couldn't see much past the patio area.

"Muffy!" she repeated again. Usually Muffy was waiting at the door when she opened it. She turned on the backyard lights, but she still couldn't see Muffy anywhere. She felt a chill down her spine, what an odd feeling, she thought. Instinctively, she knew something was wrong, but she didn't feel like going out into the dark yard alone. She closed the glass door and ran upstairs, taking the stairs two at a time, she ran into the bedroom.

"Doug, come quick!"

Doug was sound asleep. She shook him, waking him up.

"Doug, something is wrong. Muffy didn't come back."

Doug rolled over groggy and mumbled, "What?"

Alarmed she said, "It's Muffy. She's gone. She didn't come back after I let her out. She's always waiting at the door. I'm afraid something has happened to her."

"It's just a dog honey. Go to bed, don't worry about it. She'll be there tomorrow morning. Besides, there's a doghouse in the backyard, that's what it's there for. She'll be fine." He rolled over and quickly went back to sleep.

Sally was distraught. She ran her fingers through her hair, what could she do? She ran back down the stairs and opened the sliding glass door again, and went outside.

"Muffy!" The chill went down her spine again. She was torn between her fear and her concern. She backed up to the door.

"Muffy!" She called again and again, but there was nothing.

She closed the door thinking something was dreadfully wrong. She could feel it, like a sixth sense. She stood there looking out the door, paralyzed. She didn't know what to do? No matter how many things she considered, there was no answer, not tonight anyway.

Maybe in the morning she would be able think more clearly. She went to bed, but couldn't sleep. After an hour she went back downstairs and tried again, with no results. She lay down on the sofa, watching for Muffy at the glass door and fell asleep.

Photo by Lee Dygert

6

Buck went through the usual morning routine, sending the kids off to school, and Marie off to work. After everyone was on their way Buck fired up the computer and rode the net to his favorite trading site.

His favorite software company had been up every day since last Wednesday and it was time to sell. Not much chance of it going up any longer before it corrected. Take the profit and wait for it to correct and then buy it again. It was the best cash cow on the market. After it corrected, sooner or later it would go up again. The whiz kids that ran the software company knew where the future was going because they were the ones driving it there. The future of stocks was where people spent money, it's what made the stock keep going up. The more people that buy their products, the more money the company makes and the more money the company makes the greater the value of the stock. An incredibly simple concept, but not many people who buy stocks or mutual funds understand how the system works.

It was Buck's day to go to his parent's house. He went over to their place about once a week to help around the house. Dad wasn't able to do a lot of the things he once took for granted; like cleaning off the roof and the gutters. At seventy-five, a fall off the roof could easily result in a broken leg, back, hip, paralysis or even death. The roof is simply not a safe place for someone over sixty. Buck had scolded him, that kind of accident would be horrible for both him and mom. Even picking weeds in the garden resulted in days of pain for Dad these days, mostly from arthritis and less activity.

Buck was happy to be able to have the time to spend with his parents and help them out. Today Jack needed some help painting the house. It hadn't been painted for over ten years and it was beginning to look shabby. Buck loved the old house that he'd lived in for over eighteen years. It wasn't very big, but he really felt comfortable there.

Buck arrived shortly after nine in the morning. It was a nice day, the sun was trying to break out of the clouds, but it was having a hard time. The temperature was in the mid fifties. Best of all, the weatherman said that it should be an unseasonably dry spring day with the temperature going as high as seventy. As Buck got out of the car he took in a deep breath of the fresh, cool spring breeze. It smelled of evergreen trees, what a great smell.

Buck's Mother was on her hands and knees working in the flowerbed when Buck drove up the driveway. She got up as soon as she saw him and went over and gave him a big hug and a kiss.

"Oh Buck, it's so good to see you again. Thanks for coming over to help Dad with the painting."

"I'm glad to do it. I love coming over to see you and do whatever I can to help out."

"How about a cup of coffee before you get started? I made some fresh cinnamon rolls this morning just for you. I know how much you love them."

"You don't need to ask me twice if I want fresh cinnamon rolls and coffee."

They went in the house where Jack was sitting at the table with a fresh cup of coffee. He got up and they gave each other a hug. "Morning Buck, ready to do some painting?"

"Ready to roll, as soon as I get some fortification. Mom baked my favorite rolls, so I guess I had better test them."

"Did you see the late news last night? There was a cougar in a King County residential area last night. They tranquilized it and took it up into the mountains to let it go."

"No, I didn't see the news last night. Another cougar huh, they've had several in the last year or so."

"It appeared to be full grown and it looked like it was a healthy one, too."

"Seems like an odd coincidence. There's a meeting tonight at the Newtown City hall about the cougar that was in the city's maintenance yard the other day. I'm planning to go to the meeting to see what they intend to do about it."

"Well they don't belong in the city, I can tell you that for sure. To my knowledge there are only three predatory animals in the world that will stalk, kill and eat humans, the Bengal Tiger, black bears and the cougar. Brown bears, like grizzly's, have also kill and eaten humans, but I don't think they usually stalk the person. I think those incidents usually happen when the person shows up in the bear's territory. They just don't like people around and it's an opportune meal. Grizzly bears are just downright mean. Anyone who thinks they should be re-introduced anywhere should have to have one in their backyard for awhile. People who live in the city should never be in a position to make the rules for those who live in the country." Jack was winding down. "Don't get me going on that subject. Damn city slickers don't know anything about being in the woods. They think it's like the Disney movies."

He finished off his coffee and roll. "Looks like it's time for us to go to work?"

"Yep, let's do it."

"I got up early and got it all ready. All I have to do is pour the paint in the hopper and turn the switch on."

"Great, that'll speed up the job substantially."

After they'd finished for the day Buck was pretty tired. He did most of the painting while his dad fed paint to the system and did some touch-up work, Jack seemed full of energy. Buck took off his coveralls and flopped down in a big chair on the covered front porch. He remembered sitting in the same chair during hot summer nights when he was a kid. He'd learned a lot from his father sitting on that porch.

Jack came out of the house with an unopened bottle of Jack Daniel's and two small glasses. Neither Buck nor Jack drank much, but this occasion called for some painkiller. Jack poured two fingers in each glass and handed one to Buck. He sat down in his favorite chair and put the bottle on the end table. Jack raised his glass to Buck.

"Thanks for your help today Buck. I'd like to propose a toast to an old friend. To Two Hawks, may he rest in peace."

Buck raised his glass, "To Two Hawks."

Buck knew the routine, this was a Navy tradition too, a toast to fallen friends. Jack downed about half of his drink.

Jack gave Buck a big Cuban cigar and they both took a sniff down the length of the cigar, it smelled good. They made a ceremony of lighting them up. It wasn't legal to sell Cuban cigars, or any kind of Cuban goods in the United States. Canada didn't have any such restrictions on Cuban goods, and Canada wasn't far away. Jack kept a supply for special occasions. They sat there in silence for a few minutes.

Jack started, "I'm sure you won't remember Two Hawks, he was a Skykomish Indian that I had known for years. You probably remember Mary though, she was his wife. We used to go over to her place to visit occasionally when you were just a kid, maybe four or five years old. "

"Yes, I remember Mary very well. She had a son about my age. I remember playing with him when we went to visit. I'd guess four or five would be about right the first time I met them. I think his name was White Cloud. What's he doing these days?"

"Yes, it's been many years, but you have a good memory. I'm not sure what White Cloud is doing these days. I haven't been over to visit them for quite a few years now."

"When you were about four," his father continued on with his story, "I was working on to a big logging job about ten miles from here. It was a rugged forest area and the job would probably take about two years to log and then replant the harvested area again."

"About two weeks into the job one of the tree fallers disappeared one day. It was a mysterious disappearance. He and a fellow tree faller had just dropped a tree and his partner went on to check out their next tree to cut down. A few minutes later he looked back and his partner was gone. He looked around and called his name, but couldn't find him anywhere. Seemed like he'd just disappeared into thin air."

"By the time he found the log boss it was getting dark. They looked around as much as they could, calling out his name, but there was no sign of him. The next day all of the loggers went to the site and started looking for him. After about four hours one of the loggers found him. His intestines were in a neat pile about three feet from the body, which had been covered with leaves and sticks. Something had pulled the debris up from the surrounding area to hide the body. His face was eaten completely away, most of his internal organs were missing. The body had claw marks on the chest and back and it seemed pretty obvious a cougar had killed him. There were some tracks not too far from the body."

"We'd all spent most of our lives in the forest, logging and hunting, but none of us had ever seen a cougar before. Cougars are usually very solitary creatures, they stay away when people are around. There weren't many deer in the forest that year, I remember, we'd all commented about it and they're the primary diet for cougars. If they can't find deer, they'll eat whatever they can find. In this case, it was one of the loggers."

"In those days very few loggers carried a pistol, but many of them would carry a rifle with them in the forest. They would usually prop the rifle up against a tree near where they were working just in case. They'd use it for self-defense or whenever the cook needs a deer for the food supply locker. The biggest threat to the logger was bears and cougars, but first you have to see something that poses a possible danger and then have time to get the gun. In this case, they never saw the cougar."

"Bears are the most common problem for loggers in the woods. They can be very threatening. Especially when you are cutting down their home, they don't like that. Black bears lie in the trees during the day. Sometimes the base of a tree has rotted out or the tree was struck by lightening and the base of the tree is burned out inside, creating a hollow area in the base of the tree. This happens to the cedar trees a lot and the bears like to use this hollowed out space as a home."

"Cougars are different, they don't like being around people and will travel long distances to avoid humans. They're reclusive and not usually a problem. None of us ever heard of a cougar killing a human before. They are, however, very sneaky, and quiet. If they're starving, they're much more dangerous than a bear. The logger probably never knew what hit him."

"The incident spooked the rest of the loggers. The log boss decided they'd have to get it before they could continue working because once they eat a human, the human becomes a part of its normal diet. There were plenty of hunters in the bunch, but not one had ever hunted cougar. These people hunted for food, and cougar was not considered food. In fact, none of them had ever seen a cougar before, outside of a zoo. We spent the whole day hunting for it in groups of two, but nobody saw anything."

"The next morning, everyone was pretty discouraged. I told the log boss I might be able to find a solution, I had an old friend that was an Indian. Two Hawks hunted a lot and he may have some experience with cougars. Maybe he'd be able to help us."

"I went to see Two Hawks and explained the situation. He wasn't real keen on the forest being cut down, but he said that once a cougar kills and eats a human, it would keep eating people until it was killed. This dietary routine would be passed on to the cougar's offspring as the mother taught the kittens how to hunt. Eventually, it would become a danger to the Indians who hunt in the same forest areas."

"Two Hawks agreed to help us out. I spent the night with him on the reservation and the next morning we left for the logging camp. I found the log boss and introduced Two Hawks to him. We loaded our rifles and set out right away for the area where the logger's body was found."

Jack paused, took a long drag on his cigar and then slowly blew out the smoke. He watched the smoke as it curled up in the air and disappeared in the soft breeze. He refilled their glasses and took another sip.

Jack began again, "We were both carrying 30-30 lever action rifles, they were the rifle of choice back then, and we never carried pistols. Two Hawks also had a big hunting knife on his belt. Once we got to the site it took him about fifteen minutes to find the cougar tracks. There'd been so many of us walking around the area it was pretty trampled, plus the forest floor had a lot of leaves and needles making it difficult to find the tracks. He had to find an area that was muddy to get some good tracks."

"Two Hawks explained that cougar hunting was a different kind of hunting. He stopped every few minutes and looked up all around in the trees. Usually when you're hunting you're looking for colors and shapes that look out of place. You look in front and behind you, from side to side, at ground level. Cougars lay in the trees or on a rock outcrop, well above the ground on a game trail. That's why hunters and hikers rarely see them, they're always looking at ground level. You have to look up to find cougars because they like to drop down on their prey without any warning. They don't spend a lot of time on the ground unless they are going after something or when they are moving into a new hunting area in search of a new prey. This time of day a cougar would probably be lying in a tree on a big branch. They don't usually bother people. If a hunter were to pass under a tree with a cougar in it, the cougar would probably just watch with curiosity. The hunter would never know the big cat was there, watching him."

A male cougar was high in a tree watching as Two Hawks and Jack walked through the woods. The cougar was six years old and weighed about two hundred and twenty pounds, its weight was at the high end for a cougar because it had plenty of deer in its own roaming area. It came into this area just two days before, following the scent and screams a female cougar makes when in heat. When a female is in heat the screams can travel for miles, its own territory was almost five miles away. He found the female two days ago and had already mated with her about thirty times that day. He would stay in the area for four days to a week, continuing to mate frequently. They shared a meal two days ago when he first arrived in the area. A meal that she had killed, a logger.

A male cougar, like most male wild animals, will become very aggressive and possessive during mating season. They're fierce fighters if any other male animal comes into their territory at that time. He was not happy about the presence of the two men, but he been around hunters in the forest before and saw hunters shoot and kill deer. He was aware of the guns and the potential danger so he continued to watch the two men with intense interest as they traveled through the forest.

Jack thought for a moment, remembering that fateful day, "This cougar is dangerous," Two Hawks had said while studying the tracks. "It has already killed and eaten a man. To make matters worse, I haven't seen any evidence of deer. The cougar will probably be very hungry if it killed the man and was only able to feed on it one time. That means we need to be very careful."

"The tracks led us to a stream bed in a narrow ravine. The streambed was mostly sand and there were good, fresh, clean, well defined tracks. We walked up the ravine for about ten minutes and then the tracks abruptly disappeared. Two Hawks froze, and then looked up. I was behind him and I looked up the side of the ravine at the same time. The cougar was on a ledge partway up the bank with its ears pinned back, mouth open, her fangs showing and she let out a scream. We both fired at the same time as the cougar was coming off the ledge just above Two Hawks."

"She landed squarely on Two Hawks, hit twice and mortally wounded, but not dead yet. With what life she had left, she was really fighting mad. Her claws gouged into Two Hawks as he thrust his knife into the cougar's throat. The knife plunged so deep into the throat, as Two Hawks struggled with the cougar, it went all the way through to the brain."

"It all happened so fast. I chambered another round as quick as I could and shot the cougar again. It went still on top of Two Hawks and I struggled to pull it off of him. I asked if he was all right. He had some claw marks on his shoulders and a couple of fang marks on his left arm, but he was OK. I took out my handkerchief and cleaned up his wounds. We took a good look at the dead cougar then looked around some more, to make sure there wasn't any more around."

"When Two Hawks took his knife and began to gut it, I couldn't believe it. 'You're not going to eat it? Cat meat?' I'd never heard of anyone eating cat meat before. As it turned out, cat meat was pretty good, but it wasn't an animal that people usually hunted, so it wasn't a popular meat."

"He said cougar have special powers and they would have a tribal ceremony and then a feast. Cougar meat is spiritual, it makes a warrior strong. As he was gutting it, he pointed to the vulva with his knife and said it was large and swollen, indicating that she was in heat. When he finished gutting it he put it over his shoulder and we started back to the camp. She weighed over one hundred pounds and Two Hawks began to tire quickly in the rugged terrain so we stopped to take a rest and sat down on an old log."

"There was still quite a distance to go and I suggested we both carry the dead cat so we decided to make a carry. We cut off a branch and then tied the two front paws together and the two rear paws together. We put the branch between the front and rear paws so we could both carry it. After we rigged it up we sat down to rest for a few minutes. We had been sitting there for about three minutes when an owl landed on a tree branch, right in front of us. It was only about ten feet away and it was right at eye level. At the time I thought it was very unusual behavior for the owl. It looked straight at Two Hawks and we heard it say, 'Whoo,' and it flew away. It was all very strange and seemed a bit eerie to me. I looked at Two Hawks and he was as white as a sheet."

I asked, "Are you OK? You look like you're in shock."

He sat there motionless for a few minutes. I started to go over to him. He simply replied, "Today is my day to die."

"What?" I couldn't believe it.

"The owl has spoken to me. It is my day to die. The owl is a conduit between the present and the future."

"I'd known Two Hawks and his family since we were kids. I knew his tribe had many traditions and that animals were an important part of their culture and heritage, but I wasn't ready for this one."

"We sat there for a long time. It was such a blow to me that I was unable to say anything. I watched as Two Hawks took a pouch out of his pack. He opened it and took out a pinch of something, sprinkled it in front of him, and said some kind of a prayer in Indian. After about ten more minutes he got up and announced. "I am ready.""

"I stood up, a little unsteady, not knowing what to think. We shouldered the branch with the cougar between us and I was in the lead. Our rifles were slung on the opposite shoulder. As we headed back to camp I was in a sort of trance, it was like I couldn't speak."

"The forest was dense and it was rough going, carrying the cougar. We had to watch the ground every step of the way to keep from twisting an ankle from the load we were carrying. We had succeeded in killing the problem cougar and we were preoccupied, Two Hawks with his thoughts and me trying to figure out what was happening and the meaning of it all. Finally, I told Two Hawks that I didn't understand the unique incident and the significance of the owl and the revelation it had presented. I'd known Two Hawks for a long time and I wasn't ready for him to die, especially that day."

"I remember asking him why he thought it was his day to die?"

The male cougar watched intently as the two men came back through the woods, he'd heard the gunshots. He could tell the men were carrying something. When they passed directly under the tree that he was lying in, he realized that what they were carrying was his mate. He became incensed with rage and let out a hair-raising cry as he jumped out of the tree from twenty feet above the ground.

"At that exact instant a cougar jumped out of the tree we were passing under and landed squarely on Two Hawks. It sank its front claws into his back, clamped its massive jaws down on his neck and put its rear claws into his lower back. Using its razor sharp rear claws it tore huge gashes down the back of his legs. Two Hawks quickly dropped the branch carrying the dead cougar and rolled to the left trying to grab his knife. I dropped my end of the branch and un-shouldered my rifle, cocking it quickly. Just before I fired I heard a loud crunch. I shot the cougar in the forequarter, knocking it off of Two Hawks and quickly shot it two more times. When I was sure it was dead I went over to Two Hawks. It had ripped its claws down his back all the way down his legs and he was bleeding profusely. As I rolled him over his head flopped on his shoulder, his neck broken. I took his hand in mine and he blinked his eyes a couple of times before they closed for good."

Jack, who was a rugged logger and mountain man, sat there, with a tear on his cheek. It was a deep emotional scar.

Buck knew the feeling of loosing a close friend all too well. He had been to many memorial services on the aircraft carriers in the forecastle and in Navy Base Chapels for his fellow naval aviators who had been killed in aircraft accidents. Always a memorial service, never a funeral, there was nothing left for a funeral service. It was always hard to talk about any of these incidents. The hardest thing for Buck was the Aviator's Prayer. The

Aviator's Prayer was read at every memorial service he had been to on the ship's forecastle. Buck couldn't recite the Aviators Prayer. He never made it through the third line before he got too choked up to continue.

Photo by Lee Dygert

7

Steven Long hadn't shown up for work for eight days and his co-workers at the sporting goods store were beginning to worry about him. He'd only worked there for two weeks, so no one knew him very well. He didn't seem to have any close friends and he appeared to be a bit of a loner. The manager, Rick, was accustomed to people not showing up for work on time, but he hadn't shown up for work at all for over a week. Not even a phone call with an excuse. That was a bit unusual considering, and he had a paycheck waiting for him. The manager was only twenty-four years old, and he didn't have much experience in things like this. He had tried to call Steven numerous times, but all he got was a recorder.

Rick called the district manager and explained the situation. The district manager said to check his personnel file for relatives and someone to notify in case of emergency. Rick found his file and looked through the papers, it only listed his parents and they were all the way across the state, a long distance call. Long distance calls were strictly against the rules. It was a long way away and not likely that they would be any help.

Rick called his father who was at home because he was unemployed. He'd been laid off from a job he held for twenty-two years. His father was fifty-one years old and had been unemployed for two years now. A college degree, all that experience and he only had three interviews in the last two years. Each time the job had gone to a woman. There was no hope of him ever finding another decent paying job at fifty-one. The country claimed to have the lowest unemployment rate in thirty years and he couldn't even get an interview. As the store manager, Rick had seen many fifty plus year old men come in looking for work. They were unemployable, but Rick couldn't tell them that. He figured his father and mother would soon be forced to move in with him. His father asked him for a hundred dollars just last week to buy groceries for he and his mother. They hadn't been able to pay the mortgage for six months and the bank had started foreclosure proceedings. It was a sad situation for which there didn't seem to be an answer.

He explained the situation to his father and asked for some advice. His father said to call the young man's parents and forget about the long distance charges, they were justifiable. If they haven't heard from him and they don't know where he is, go to his residence yourself and see if you can find him. If you can't, call the sheriff and explain it to him. Ask the sheriff to check out his disappearance.

He called Steven's parents and told them that Steven hadn't shown up for work for eight days. The parents didn't seem to be concerned. Steven did unusual things because he was obsessed with becoming an Olympic team member, implying that he'd probably show up for work in a few days. They told Rick that Steven worked very hard trying to be the best competitor so that he could make the Olympic team. They were very proud of his accomplishments, even if they didn't get to see him much anymore.

He called the sheriff in Newtown and explained that Steven hadn't shown up for work for eight days now and they were concerned. The manager went further in saying that there was no answer to the phone at his apartment, and he'd left messages but he hadn't returned the call. He explained that he called Steven's parents, who hadn't heard from him either. Could the sheriff please check it out?

The sheriff agreed to send out a deputy and would get back to him with the results.

The deputy first tried to call Steven's home phone number but he didn't get an answer there either. Next he went to Steven's apartment to check it out. When there was no answer at the door, he got the apartment manager to unlock the door and both went inside. Everything in the apartment seemed normal, relatively neat for a mid-twenty year old, single male, no signs of foul play. As they were leaving the next-door neighbor came home.

The deputy asked the neighbor, "Do you know Steven Long?"

"Yes, I've known Steven for two years."

"When did you see Steven last?"

"I think it was Sunday afternoon, about a week ago, around four. He was on his way to run in the National Forest about ten miles away, at Cross Point, for a work out. He goes up there two or three times a week. Says it's beautiful up there. It's his favorite place to run. He's an Olympic hopeful you know. Last I heard he's in the top ten competitors for the triathlon."

"Interesting, that's the same day that he was last at work. Is it normal for him to disappear for a week at a time?"

"No, not that I can remember. In fact, I think he would have said something to me if he planned to be away for this long. His next triathlon competition isn't until late next month and it's in Hawaii. I usually see him every 2-3 days and I'm pretty sure he would have told me where he was going."

"Does he have a girlfriend or a companion he hangs around with regularly?"

"No."

"Do you remember what he was wearing when he left to go workout?"

The neighbor gave him a good physical description of Steven. The deputy thanked him for his help and headed back to the station. On his way he thought about how he should handle this. He was somewhat familiar with the area where Steven was going to run. It was primarily a tree farm area, but he hadn't been up there for at least ten years. He used to hunt deer up in that area when he was younger. More importantly, it was out of their jurisdiction.

At the station the deputy told the Sheriff what he found out. The Sheriff checked the area map and confirmed it to be in the Skoko County sheriff's jurisdiction. That'd be Sheriff Mitchell, whom he hadn't seen for about three years. He went to the computer and looked up Steven Long's vehicle information, for the color, make, year, and license number. He ran a standard check on the vehicle, but it wasn't on the hot list, not reported lost or stolen, and it wasn't listed as abandoned. He checked the local hospitals to see if he'd been admitted or had been there, but there was no results.

He picked up the phone and called Mitch to explain the situation. He gave him Steven Long's description plus the vehicle information and asked if his office would check it out. Sheriff Tate had seen situations like this before, his gut feeling was that the results wouldn't be good when they finally came in.

Buck was returning from his afternoon jog, which was really more like a fast walk today. He painted all morning, figuring that was plenty of exercise, and he also had a couple of drinks with his dad on the porch after the painting. He didn't feel much like running, but wanted to keep the routine going so walking seemed like a better way to go. He was almost home when he saw Frank in his front yard. He'd just finished mowing the lawn and edging and was sweeping the grass off the walkway as Buck walked past.

"Hi Frank, beautiful day isn't it? Did your cat turn up yet?"

"No, and it ain't like her to be away so long. I'm worried something is wrong with her, maybe she's sick."

"Well, cats sometimes wander off for days. Hopefully, she'll be back soon," Buck called over his shoulder as he continued to walk.

"By the way Buck, could you keep your kids out of my yard? They were out playing last weekend at nine fifteen, making all kinds of noise. I go to bed at nine every night."

"Yes, I already talked to them Frank. They assured me that they would stay out of your yard. They shouldn't be running through your yard, but hey, they are kids you know. Kids do play and make a lot of noise. Nine fifteen to them is hardly a late hour. I'll remind them every week or so."

As he walked up his driveway Sally was picking up her mail. "Hi Sally."

"Hi Buck, have you seen our dog Muffy today?"

"No, can't say that I have."

"I let her out last night around ten o'clock to do the evening thing before I went to bed and she never came back. I've been letting her out about the same time every evening since we moved here. She always comes back in about fifteen minutes. I hope she's OK. She's never been missing for a whole day before and I don't know what to do."

"I'll keep an eye out for her. I'm sure she'll turn up soon. Have you called the pound? Maybe she's there. See you around," he called over his shoulder as he walked up to the house.

He couldn't help thinking that this may not be a coincidence. He'd been talking to a neighbor down the street last week who just lost a dog the night before, the same way. He let the dog out in the late evening and it hadn't come back. After a week he presumed the dog was lost. In fact, another neighbor only about a block away in the opposite direction from his house lost a cat only last week. She distributed flyers to all the neighbors and the local stores. To top it off, Frank's cat was now missing. Odd that so many pets had disappeared in such a short time, he thought.

The school bus stopped at the street and the kids spilled out in all directions. Rob came running up the driveway.

"Hey Rob, how was your day at school? I expected you to be riding home with Eric. Where is he?"

"Eric had to stay after school again to work on a project and I have a soccer game in half hour."

"Yeah, I was planning to go watch the game. How come you're home then?"

"I forgot to take my uniform to school again today, and I had to come home to get it."

"You forgot your uniform yesterday too.   You should've called me, I would've brought it to you."

"I didn't think of that. I've got to get back to school fast or the coach won't let me play today."

"OK. Get your uniform on and let's go!"

Photo by Lee Dygert

8

Buck was preparing dinner early so he could go to the town meeting tonight, mostly out of curiosity because he wasn't very fond of meetings. They were usually such a waste of time and they could go on for hours. Fifteen minutes of meat, and hours of B.S. That didn't happen in the Navy, people had things to do. Sitting around talking about it all day didn't accomplish anything. Odds were that if there were one hundred people at a meeting, then there were one hundred different opinions or ideas. No one would come to an agreement on anything. What they need is a person in charge with some backbone that could analyze the situation, make a decision, and get on with it.

Buck was civic minded, he did volunteer work at the local middle school occasionally. He'd struck up a friendship with a sixth grade teacher when Eric was in his class. He continued to help in the classroom on special occasions even after his children had all gone through the school. Mr. Hargrave, a strong candidate for 'Teacher of the Year,' was firm, yet fair, had good control in the classroom, was interesting and the students had a strong respect for him. Buck helped him out doing woodworking projects with the students and with the annual one week of self- improvement for the students. This so called 'Ropes Course' was designed to make them work together to solve problems, to develop teamwork and build self-confidence. Buck enjoyed helping the kids learn teamwork, especially because it was all done outside, even when it was raining.

He also taught a course for the local school district similar to the one he taught at the university, only it was a very compressed version. This was a one-week field trip for all sixth graders in the school district. The facility for the outdoor education course was an old Civilian Conservation Corps camp in the Cascade Mountains run by the U.S. Forest Service. The instructors were all the student's regular teachers, with a few specialty subject instructors, like Buck. The classes were three hours long, one in the morning and one in the afternoon. All the classes covered different outdoors subjects, including Buck's survival class. The students lived in barrack style cabins with a counselor for each six students. The counselors were high school juniors and seniors who had gone through the same program when they were sixth graders in the same school district. The instructors lived in an adjacent housing area for the week, where their accommodations were, Spartan at best, very old mobile homes. Everyone ate together at the dining hall, which was staffed by the Forest Service. It was a fun, but tiring, week for all and a lifelong educational experience for the students.

Buck taught the students what they could eat in the forest and what not to eat, where to find water and how to purify it, how to read a compass, and how to use a map. The most important thing he taught them was how to build a shelter and a fire, and prevent hypothermia. In the northwest, hypothermia was the most dangerous thing that a person had to deal with in a survival situation. Finally, he taught them how to find their way out of the forest if they weren't rescued in three days. It was the favorite class of the week for most of the students.

As he worked on dinner the television was on the evening news, he turned it up while he peeled the potatoes. The on-site reporter was in Newtown at the elementary school.

"A cougar was sighted outside the fence at Von Elementary School in Newtown this afternoon. All the children were hurried inside and the sheriff was called. When Sheriff Tate and a deputy arrived the cougar was gone."

As they searched the area Sheriff Tate wondered if this was mass hysteria. If it was, it was spreading fast. He figured it was getting so much high level attention he'd better stay personally involved instead of letting the deputies handle it. They didn't find a cougar or any sign of one, but he told Ms. Wilson, the school principal, that he would leave one of the deputies there for the rest of the day. He'd discuss the matter with the mayor before the meeting tonight. The meeting was already scheduled because of the cougar sighting in the city maintenance yard yesterday morning.

Buck thought, this should add to the excitement at tonight's meeting. If nothing else, it would be entertaining. Most likely it was the same yellow Labrador retriever they saw at the soccer game last night when everyone went into a panic.

Sally was watching the same newscast. A cougar on the school grounds where her children attended school didn't seem like a good idea, but it was probably just a big dog. Everybody in town was going crazy since the cougar was seen in the maintenance yard yesterday, it was most likely all hype. Everyone was trying to build support to get all the wild animals eradicated from town. They complained that the raccoons raided their trashcans, spread garbage all over the yard, and constantly ate their dog and cat food they left outside. To support their complaint they said raccoons carry rabies. Sally thought, these people needed to sit down and watch the animals. It's like a religious experience, they're wonderful to watch. People are too busy, they need to stop and smell the roses. She thought to herself, we'll be there at the meeting tonight to bring some reality back to Newtown. We want it to stay natural, the animals were here first, leave them alone. She continued to formulate her speech for the cause of the cougars in her mind.

The town meeting was well attended. The council wisely chose to have the meeting at the high school gymnasium instead of the council chambers. The events of the last two days developed considerable community interest. There were over two hundred fifty people in attendance for the meeting. This was going to be good, thought Buck, it might even be worth a price of admission.

Buck took a seat and looked up at the city council management team. There were nine people sitting at the official's table in front of the gymnasium bleachers, seven women and two men. One of the men was the sheriff, the other was the city financial manager. The number of women vs. the number of men struck him immediately. The mayor, city manager, city manager's assistant, city clerk, and the city council were all women.

The mayor began the meeting about fifteen minutes after the scheduled start time as people continued to straggle into the gymnasium.

"We are here tonight to discuss the possible presence of a cougar in our community."

The rumblings began immediately as the audience displayed their discontent. The comments boiled down to, "What do you mean 'possible' cougar? It's been seen twice in the last two days!"

The mayor tried to remain calm, "The sheriff did see a cougar at the city maintenance yard yesterday morning. The cougar apparently had killed and was eating a raccoon. There is also the possibility of a cougar sighting near Von Elementary School today. This sighting is a little sketchy and it hasn't been confirmed as a true cougar sighting. There is the possibility that it could've been a large tan colored dog."

The crowd began to complain again. One woman stood up.

"I'm keeping my children at home until this cougar is caught. I'm not going to have my children eaten on the school grounds!" The crowd mumbled their support of keeping the children at home.

By the time the meeting had been going on for an hour Buck knew that nothing was going to happen tonight.

Sally and her group from the Naturalist Club were conferring. Sally was waiting for a good opportunity to get up and speak on behalf of the club. The other members that were present were vocal in expressing their feelings whenever the crowd started complaining.

The crowd was becoming hostile.

The mayor leaned over to one of the council members and they talked for a minute. She stood up.

"The city managers have decided that all the city schools will be closed tomorrow. We will now go into private session to discuss our options. We'll plan to have another town meeting here again tomorrow night at seven o'clock."

The city managers then all stood up in unison and walked out of the gym. The crowd was obviously not happy.

Buck thought this was all predictable. Tomorrow night would be a must attend though and he got up and went home.

The city managers and council went back to city hall and had a private session. Sitting around the long table in the city managers conference room the mayor starting off the meeting.

"It's obvious we need to do something. A cougar could easily kill someone, but there is some in the audience who want us to leave the animal alone and not to hurt it. The two percent of them that are animal rights activists make about ninety percent of the noise. What do you think we should do?"

Sheriff Tate said, "This is too big of a problem for us to handle with our staff. To top it off, none of us know anything about cougars. If one shows up and we get there fast enough we can tranquilize or shoot it, but if we need to go out hunting for it that's a completely different story. I'm going to require some expert advice and assistance if it comes to a hunting expedition."

The city manager said, "I've been contacted, just today, by a retired forest ranger that is now a consultant. He saw the reports on television and offered his services. He said he is very familiar with cougars and is a specialist in removing problem animals from inhabited areas. He gave me two references and I've already spoken with both of them. They were both city managers from eastern Washington and they said he got rid of their cougars in a few days."

It was all happening so fast, but they couldn't afford to hesitate, not with the possibility that it could take a life. Each council member thought they needed to have more time to research everything they wanted to know, but they all agreed they needed professional help. They also agreed that they did not have time to do a lot of research and have more meetings and draw it out, like they did most issues. This problem needed an immediate solution. The council chair said she'd set it up for him to be at the city meeting tomorrow night.

The cougar started roaming around the houses in the new development area of Newtown as soon as it got dark. The yards around the houses had proven to be a good place to find a meal. Many of the houses had cats and dogs, which were frequently let out in the evening. He killed a dog last night and it was a good meal, but a hundred pound cougar could easily eat a dog every day. The one it ate last night made only a meager meal and he was ready for greater sustenance.

At nine forty-five Bill Fox was ready to retire for the evening. He'd worked for the Newtown Fire Department for ten years. He loved the town, it was such a beautiful place to live and to raise the children. He was about to get into bed when his wife asked.

"Dear, did you put the trash out? Tomorrow is trash collection day."

"Oh no, I forgot, thanks for the reminder. Guess I'd better do it now, if I wait till tomorrow morning it'll be just my luck they'll come early, before I get up."

He was already in his pajamas, but he figured, who'd see him at this hour? He emptied all the wastebaskets from around the house and went out to the garage. The container was full, so he put his foot in and pushed it down so he could get the rest of the trash into the can. It was a messy job, especially in his pajamas and slippers. He secured the lid tightly to keep the raccoons from raiding the trash. He pushed the button to the garage door opener and it began to work its way up.

As the cougar walked around the perimeter of a house down the street he was startled by a loud noise. He stopped, hunkered down low to the ground, watching and listening to determine what the sound was. It was coming from down the street and his keen night vision revealed a man wheeling a trashcan down the driveway.

Bill felt a little chill as he pulled the trashcan to the street. Funny he thought, it wasn't really that cold this evening. As he walked back up the driveway, he saw a soda can lying next to the garage. When he bent over to pick it up the chill hit him again.

The cougar slowly began to stalk the man in the dark. He watched intently as the man walked up the driveway, bent over to pick up something, and then headed back to the street.

Bill put the can in the trashcan and then headed back up the driveway.

When the man started walking back up the driveway a second time the cougar started running toward him. When he was only forty feet away, the man went into the garage. The cougar was cautious now because of being trapped in a garage before. It walked to the front of the garage and saw the man. A noise startled it and he jumped back as the garage door began to come down. The cougar backed off, it wasn't about to be trapped in a garage again. He continued walking around on his search from house to house looking for prey.

As Bill walked up the stairs to bed he had a strange feeling that something was not right, but he couldn't imagine what it was. He guessed he was too tired.

Blake was stoned, he'd been smoking marijuana since he got home from work. It was nearly midnight and he needed to get to bed. He'd never be able to get up for work if he didn't get to sleep soon. Fortunately, he didn't have to be at work until ten o'clock. He worked in a clothing store at the local mall.

Blake was house-sitting his parent's house while they were away for the winter. His parents were snowbirds, people who went south in the winter to Southern California, Arizona, or New Mexico to get away from the cold and wet winters of the northwest. Blake's parents went to Arizona for the winter every year and they were due back in two weeks. He needed to find an apartment soon. He got up to go to bed, but his dog was standing at the door, it wanted out. Oh crap, he thought, I can't walk you now. The rottweiler scratched the door again. Blake let 'Devil' out the front door and sat down on the sofa. It wasn't long before he slumped down and fell asleep.

The rottweiler walked around the front yard, sniffing and leaving urine at each spot. It caught an unusual scent that it didn't like and pinned its ears back.

The cougar watched as the door opened and out came the dog. This looked like his next meal. He crouched down, ears back, mouth open, and fangs at the ready and made a dash for the dog.

The rottweiler sensed something and turned just in time to see the cougar coming toward him. He knew an attack was coming and bristled, growling, facing his attacker, ready for the fight.

As the cougar pounced on the dog, the dog lit into the cougar. The dog got a good grip on the upper section of the left front leg. The cougar clamped its jaws down on the dog's back and put its right front claws up under the dog. He dug his claws into the soft underside of the dog and ripped them down the dog's belly. The dog's intestines quickly spilled out on the driveway as the cougar clamped his jaws shut like a vice and shook his head from side to side breaking the dog's spine. The whole battle was over in less than twenty seconds. He easily dragged the dog off into the woods to find a secluded place to feed. He found a good tree and jumped up on the trunk dragging the dog up to a branch that was big enough for him to lie down while eating the dog. Taking prey up into a tree to be consumed is not normal cougar behavior. It is adapted behavior when cougars are living near human habitation. The only other big cats that take prey up into trees to feed are the cheetah and leopard. They do it to keep other predators, like lions and hyenas, from stealing their food.

The next morning when Blake woke up on the sofa he realized he had let Devil out the night before. Since the dog wasn't lying on the floor next to him, as usual, he figured the dog was still outside. He opened the front door and called, "Devil."

"Devil!"

He was nowhere in sight so he went out to look around. As he was walking around the house he noticed something was on the driveway. He went over to it to get a better look and saw the pile of intestines and a patch of dog fur. He quickly realized that what he was looking at was 'Devil', or what was left of him. A wave of nausea swept over him and he began to throw up. Falling to his hands and knees, he retched for ten minutes. He couldn't call the police, they might want to come into the house. With all the drug paraphernalia lying around there was no way he was going to call the cops. He needed to get the place cleaned up before his parents got home, but it wouldn't be today.

Getting up slowly, he went into the garage and retrieved a shovel. Unsteadily he returned to the kill site and scooped up the dog's guts. He carried the mass, spilling over the edges of the shovel, over to what passed for a flowerbed, dug a hole and buried the guts. He got the hose and cleaned off the driveway, he was really shaken up. Whatever it was that did this to his dog he didn't want to know. He went into the house and lit up a joint. This was going to be a bad day. He called work and told them he'd be out sick.

Photo by Lee Dygert

9

Sheriff Mitchell sent a deputy out to Cross Point to look around for Steven Long and his car. The deputy wasn't real keen on going way out there by himself, but they were short handed at the office today and didn't have enough deputies to send out two. When he got there he found Steven's car without any trouble. It was parked in an area surrounded by evergreen trees and the car was locked with no sign of foul play. He radioed in to the dispatcher that the car was there. He walked around the area looking for Steven or any footprints that might lead him to Steven, but found nothing at all. He decided to look around a little longer and found a trail that looked like a probable way Steven would've taken for a run. It was an inviting trail, actually an old forest road with a spectacular canopy of tree branches arching over the trail. It was enchanting, so he started down the trail and kept on looking. After walking for about fifteen minutes he heard an unusual clicking sound that sent a chill down his spine, warning him that something wasn't right. Now he really wished he wasn't there by himself, but the area seemed so quiet and serene he convinced himself to keep on going.

Guardedly, he walked until he reached the meadow. It was so beautiful and mesmerizing it was almost like a place right out of a fairy tale. It's such a quaint place and so close to the city limits, he thought. He walked to the end of the meadow passing under a huge tree that looked to be well over a hundred years old. As he searched the area he saw what looked like blood on the trail. Examining it closer he saw that something fairly large had been dragged up the hill. He followed the drag trail for about five minutes and emerged from a narrow trail into an open area. There lay a human body or what little was left. It was mostly bones, a skeleton that had been licked clean of all the meat. The bones looked like they were still wet, it was all very fresh. There were numerous tracks around the body. They were big prints, without any claw prints in front of the toe pads. The main pad was very large, and the prints were almost round. They were nearly five inches across. He figured they must be cat prints, big cat prints. He drew out his nine-millimeter service pistol and cocked it. He looked around, but didn't see or hear anything. Now he really wished he wasn't there alone. He reached up to his shoulder and pressed the two-way radio attached to his shirt.

"Dispatch, this is Deputy Moore, over"

There was no response. He was a long way from the base station and there were a lot of mountains and trees between them. After making two more attempts, he decided he wasn't going to get through. He started back down the trail holding his pistol in front of him. His eyes were darting everywhere, listening intently. Very nervous, he kept checking over his shoulder behind him.

A juvenile cougar lay in a tree at the edge of the open area near the skeleton. It watched the deputy as he examined the skeleton. The cougar now looked at the man as a possible meal. As the deputy walked back down the trail to the meadow the juvenile cougar effortlessly dropped out of the tree and began to stalk him. He tracked the deputy, taking slow, quiet steps, and staying well behind him out of sight until he instinctively knew when to attack.

The deputy came off the hill and back onto the service road at the edge of the meadow. He felt safer now that he was back on the service road and relaxed his grip on his pistol, letting it fall to his side. He tried the radio again, but there was still no response.

The mother cougar laid in the old oak tree watching as the deputy walked under the tree. Two of her kittens had departed, gone out on their own. Of the three she had left, two were still malnourished.

The deputy thought that it was such a beautiful place, but he couldn't shake the feeling of death close by. He had a terrible sinking feeling and found that his thoughts were turning to his childhood and very specific things he did as a child. It was like he was seeing a movie of his life and all the unique events that happened to him. He saw himself hitting the homerun that won the game for his

Little League baseball team when he was eleven years old. He saw himself in the chapel standing next to his wife at their wedding. He saw himself at his father's funeral and remembered the incredible sorrow he felt.

This was weird, he thought, like he was in some kind of trance. He shook his head trying to make it go away, but it just played faster. This made him extremely nervous. He hastened his pace. Shortly thereafter, he thought he heard something behind him. Quickly he turned around to look over his shoulder.

The mother cougar was coming toward him at a full run, then she jumped at him. She was about ten feet away and as he raised his gun another cougar jumped off a ledge beside the trail and hit him from the side. The gun went off into the ground as the juvenile cougar ripped into his side. Now two cougars were on him, making it impossible to get his pistol in position to fire. One cougar ripped its claw down his right arm, tearing the pistol out of his hand. As he struggled he felt severe pain everywhere. The mother cougar clamped her massive jaws shut on his throat. His eyes bulged out as the pain got worse and he struggled, trying to push the cats off of him. She had cut off his windpipe and he could not breathe. He took his hands and grabbed each side of her jaws trying to loosen her grip on his throat. Her jaws were closed like a vice, they wouldn't budge. The mother cougar twisted and pulled violently, shaking her head and ripping a gaping hole in his throat.

The mother cougar grabbed him by the head, taking his entire head in her mouth. She dragged the deputy's body, between her front legs, back up the same hill, with her three offspring following close behind her. When they reached the clearing they began to tear the body apart. The healthiest of the three remaining kittens snarled at the other two kittens and made them back off while it ripped big chunks of flesh from the leg and swallowed it. The other two kittens sat back and waited. When the aggressive kitten was full she turned away and walked into the woods. Now weighing about one hundred pounds and almost ready to go into her first heat, she felt the pull of nature and headed north, deeper in the Cascade Mountains, leaving her family behind. She started out at a fast pace covering about five miles an hour.

Later that day, as the sun was going down, she was crossing the Skykomish Indian Nation land. Two Indians were out hunting for deer and Little Bear saw the cougar as it crossed their path, about two hundred yards in front of them.

"Look," he said to White Cloud, "Swawa," (the Indian name for cougar).

White Cloud replied, "This is a bad sign for deer hunting. It's not likely we'll find any deer now. The swawa will have them very nervous. Let's head south to hunt in the river area."

"We could go after the swawa."

"No, swawa hunting is only for very special occasions, unless it has killed someone. Then it must be killed to keep it from killing more people."

By two o'clock that afternoon the deputy on duty hadn't heard from Deputy Moore since his initial report of finding Steven Long's car, this wasn't normal procedure. The deputy had tried to call him numerous times with no answer and he decided it was time to inform Sheriff Mitchell. When Sheriff Mitchell heard there had been no contact from the deputy for over two hours he got two more deputies and drove out to the site. On arrival to the parking lot the Sheriff and his deputies found both vehicles. There didn't appear to be anything unusual, no sign of violence or foul play. Sheriff Mitchell used the car radio to call in. The car radio was more powerful than the portable radios they carried with them and the response came right back. He reported his findings and told the duty deputy to send two more deputies out to the scene.

When the backup unit arrived, it was the two newest deputies to the department. One, a woman, was one of only two women in the department. The Sheriff had second thoughts about taking two inexperienced deputies on this mission, especially the woman, but there wasn't time to gct anyone else to the site. He figured he needed at least four deputies to go out there safely, not knowing what to expect. The Sheriff was from the old school, law enforcement was not woman's work. He'd been against hiring the women in the first place, but they'd scored the highest on the civil service tests, and he didn't have any choice.

The five of them started down the trail when Sheriff Mitchell stopped. He thought for a second and then told the deputies to go back and get their shotguns. As they walked down the service road and into the meadow area Sheriff Tate said.

"This is really a spectacularly beautiful place. I can see why Steven Long liked running here."

They continued along the trail until they reached the end of the meadow where they came across fresh blood on the trail. They quickly found drag marks going up the hill into the forest. Sheriff Mitchell drew out his nine-millimeter pistol. The deputies followed suit readying their weapons. Tate motioned for them to spread out.

He whispered, "I'll stay on the trail, two of you go out to each side of me and spread out about ten feet apart. Pay attention and be careful. We don't know what we're getting into here, but Deputy Moore may be in trouble. If he is we need to find him fast."

Sheriff Mitchell started up the game trail. They were all very quiet, being careful not to make any noise warning anyone or anything of their approach. In about five minutes they came to an open area. They all arrived at the edge of the clearing at the same time. Everyone drew in their breath sharply.

"Oh my God," they each thought.

In the clearing were three cougars, feeding on what appeared to be a human and there was a human skeleton nearby. The cougars were so focused on feeding and making so much noise eating they didn't hear the team approach. The sheriff and the deputies all began firing at the same time. The shotguns all used double ought buck, for heavy-duty knock down power, and all three cougars were literally blown apart in a matter of seconds.

They went over to the body, but there wasn't much left of their comrade. He'd been eaten all over the face, the internal organs, shoulders, buttocks, and the big muscles on the back of the legs. The intestines were laying in a neat pile about three feet from the body. It was a gruesome sight. The torn shreds of a uniform were next to the body, the deputy's shoes were still on the feet, untouched. A piece of material held a nametag, which read, DEPUTY MOORE. After surveying the scene the new deputy's stomach started to burn and churn. Moments later he lost his lunch. The sound, and smell started a chain reaction, and the woman deputy followed suit. They all thought to themselves, it could have been me lying there. It looked like he didn't even have a chance. The other three took off their hats and held them over their hearts.

Sadly, as he bowed his head, Sheriff Mitchell said a prayer over the body.

"Dear Lord, please take care of our fallen officer, Deputy Moore. He was a fine man, a dedicated officer, and a family man, may he rest in peace."

He could hear the others softly sniffling, knowing he'd find tears on their faces if he glanced up.

Within days of the deaths, autopsies of the killed cougars were performed. The autopsies revealed DNA evidence from the intestinal tract of each cat that matched the DNA of both Steven Long and deputy sheriff Moore.

Photo by Lee Dygert

10

Buck arrived at the high school gymnasium at six forty-five and visited with some of the neighbors while they waited for the meeting to get started. At seven o'clock the high school gymnasium was packed to overflowing. All the bleachers were full and people were standing along the sides, completely filling the gym.

Sally was there again with her Naturalist Club members. They were all up in the bleachers and Sally was impatient for her chance to speak out. They were really ready for a fight tonight.

The city management team came in together and sat down at the table that was set-up in front of the bleachers. The mayor had no idea what was going to happen. The mayor felt uncomfortable. She had been so busy she had

only been able to talk to Mr. Woods for a few minutes
before the meeting got started. She was a little unsure
what he was going to say. She only knew what the council
chair explained to her during their phone call earlier this
afternoon. She was told that Mr. Woods would be there
tonight and wouldn't have much time before the meeting
to talk with her.

The mayor stepped up to the podium and tested the
microphone by gently tapping the top. Satisfied it was
working fine she began, "This meeting tonight is a follow
up on last night's meetings. The city council and I had a
closed session meeting last night after our meeting here to
discuss the problem of a cougar in our neighborhood. We
have with us this evening Mr. Woods, a retired forest
ranger who is now a consultant on problem animals in
populated areas."

Mr. Woods stepped up to the podium, "Good evening
ladies and gentlemen. As the mayor said, I'm a retired
forest ranger and I now do consulting work concerning
problem animals. In the last ten years we've seen a
troubling increase with problem animals in cities. First,
I'll give you a little background on the problem."

"About ten years ago there was a major
psychological change in the society across the country
concerning hunting and wild animals in general. The
change being that hunting was no longer needed to
provide food for the family. In fact, it was no longer
considered acceptable to kill deer so consequently there
became fewer and fewer hunters. This psychology pretty
much swept across the whole country. Laws were then
changed to reduce the number of deer being killed each
year. This was accomplished by reducing the number of
hunting days to only two to four days per year. The
results were predictable to me at that time. Over the years
the deer population increased, slightly in the beginning,
but by 1994, it was common for deer to be seen in the

city. Previous to this change in psychology, having deer in the city was unheard of."

"This happened for two reasons. The first, and most important, was that deer hunting had become less popular. This meant that fewer deer were being killed each year. Therefore, the population grew at an exponential rate. Second, the deer spread out and ended up in the city, where food was plentiful. Well-tended gardens of flowers and vegetables were everywhere, and the deer flourished. More importantly, there weren't any predators. The only threat was the automobile, because the deer hadn't developed a fear of cars. Some of the deer population had been reduced by being hit by vehicles, but nowhere near the numbers that were killed by hunters."

"This is where your problem comes in, it's directly related to the deer in your yard. Deer are the primary source of food for cougars. One cougar will kill and eat a deer about every five to seven days, if there is sufficient deer population in its roaming area to support this kind of diet. As the deer population exploded in the 1990's, so did the cougar population, that's the way nature works. Whenever there is an abundance of food, the animal that consumes the food begins to reproduce more often and they have larger numbers of offspring. Now, ten years after the new laws went into effect, the cougars are beginning to have more frequent and larger litters. In the last few years the cougar population has continued to expand."

"As the young cougars become mature enough to go out on their own they are faced with a dilemma. The entire existing predator habitat in the wild is inhabited with cougars or bears. These predators are very solitary and possessive and they won't share areas. Young cougars leave their mother between twelve and twenty-four months of age. If the young cougar goes into an area that is occupied, it must either fight or leave the area. When it chooses to fight the more mature and experienced predator, the younger one is usually killed and eaten. Consequently, the young and inexperienced animals usually instinctively avoid the fight and flee. The only unoccupied habitat left is in the areas immediately adjacent to housing developments. Mature cougars are shy and reclusive, they avoid human contact, but the young cougars are forced to live near people to survive. Because of this, the new generation is loosing its fear of humans and this is a very dangerous evolutionary change. Cougars are the most efficient predators in the United States and they will not allow themselves to starve to death."

"Cougars are carnivores, they only eat meat. When they are hungry and can't find deer, they will eat nearly anything they can catch, usually rabbits, rats, mice, porcupines, squirrels, raccoons, and possum. If they 're hungry enough, and can't find anything else, they'll even eat skunks. In some areas the excessive cougar populations have completely decimated the food supply in their roaming area and there is nothing left for them to eat. The result is the cougars are following the deer population into the city. This is a normal, predictable occurrence. Like the cave men, the cougar must follow its food supply."

"Then the whole cycle repeats itself. The cougar consume the deer in the city, and then look for an alternate food source. Since there are fewer squirrels, rabbits, and raccoons in the city, they disappear fairly quickly. The next food source is cats and dogs."

"Cougars are normally very shy and reclusive. Up until the last few years it was a very rare occasion for anyone to see a cougar. As the food source begins to dry up, the cougars become more aggressive. They're not concerned about being around humans when they need to find food. About this time neighborhood cats and dogs begin to disappear and we start to have more and more frequent sightings of cougars."

The Newtown deputy sheriff on duty took the call. It was Sheriff Mitchell from Skoko County and he needed to speak with Sheriff Tate. The deputy explained that Sheriff Tate was in a very important town management meeting concerning a cougar in town and he didn't want to be disturbed unless it was a life or death situation.

"This is very important and it could easily turn into a life threatening situation, since you had a cougar in your city maintenance yard this week. Break into the meeting and have him call me ASAP," and hung up. The deputy figured he wasn't going to argue with Sheriff Mitchell, after all, he knew what was going on so he paged Sheriff Tate.

When his pager went off he thought, 'this had better be good. I know I told the deputy not to bother me tonight.' The sheriff leaned over to the mayor and explained to her that he just received an urgent page. He got up and hurried out of the gymnasium.

He went out to his car to make the call to the deputy. Times like this he wished the city would get him a cellular phone. The city wouldn't spend a dime on anything it considered frivolous, clinging to the small town mentality. He approached the council only two months ago about purchasing cell phones, but they considered cell phones an unnecessary and extravagant expense. Sheriff Tate used the two-way radio in his car to make the call to the deputy on duty. The deputy told him that Sheriff Mitchell wanted him to call ASAP.

"Dial him up and patch the call through on this radio. I'll standby here until I can talk with Mitch."

The deputy on duty thought that this wasn't a secure way to make the call, but the Sheriff made the rules, so he did as he was told.

"Sheriff Mitchell here."

"Hi Mitch, this is Tate. What's up?"

Mitch told him they found Steven Long's body and then informed him that one of his deputies was killed in the process. Both of them had been killed and eaten by three cougars, a mother and two juveniles. He and his deputies killed all three of them, but he was suspicious there might be more cougars, because there were so many cougar tracks in the area.

Tate said, "Mitch, I appreciate the call and I'm sorry you lost a deputy. Anything I can do to assist?"

"No, but thanks."

Sheriff Tate went back to the meeting to find Mr. Woods still talking.

"This is where you are now. I've done some checking around the neighborhood this afternoon. There's more than a few dogs and cats that have disappeared in the last two weeks. I searched around the trails that go throughout your neighborhood and found cougar tracks and markings. In fact, there's so many signs, that I'm suspicious you may have a cougar on the west side of town and another one on the east side."

"The next food source is what you need to be concerned about. A dog or cat is usually only enough to sustain a cougar for one day. Once the cougar has depleted all the available dogs and cats it won't voluntarily allow itself to starve to death. There are plenty of people in town and they're easy prey for a cougar, especially children and the elderly. Cougars have killed and eaten humans recently under circumstances similar to yours."

"In Colorado last month, a high school teacher went jogging on a trail just behind the high school leaving his car in the parking lot. When he didn't show up to teach classes the next day, they went looking for him. He was in excellent physical condition, but when they found him he'd been killed and partially eaten. He simply didn't have a chance against the cougar. Even an unarmed, highly trained, professional football player wouldn't have a chance against a cougar, if the cougar was really hungry and made a surprise attack from the rear."

"Incidents like this make the front page of the local paper, but only occasionally does it make the national news. It's rare to find a report indicating the victim was eaten. People don't want to read about humans being eaten, it's a scary thing, so the media deliberately excludes these facts. It's also a problem in the local area, people don't want to hear that a wild animal ate a neighbor. The local and national media avoid reporting this information."

"Here in Washington State, we have a unique situation. A high percentage of the state is tree-farming area and this is prime habitat for cougars. It's also an area where deer thrive, so the cougars do well here. The 1996 state law prohibiting the hunting of cougar and bear with dogs further complicates the situation. Until three years ago hunters used dogs to find the cougars and bears keeping the population in check. The new law stopped this practice and has exacerbated the cyclical expansion in the population of these predators. My thirty years of experience tells me we should anticipate an increasing problem with both of these animals intruding into populated areas, with the cougar being the most serious threat to people. "

"In 1995, there were 247 confirmed cougar and human encounters. In 1996, there were 495 encounters, and in 1997, there were 563 cougar and human encounters in Washington state. These are statistics the Fish and Wildlife Department has collected. From my experience in similar situations over the past three years, I anticipate the available dog and cat supply in this town is about depleted. I'd expect there to be a human casualty here soon, most likely a child."

Mr. Woods took a series of questions from the audience. It was obvious they were all very scared. After the questions stopped, Mr. Woods sat down. The mayor stood up and said the city managers would go into private session and discuss the evening's revelations.

The crowd got to their feet and demanded that something be done right now. People were yelling.

"We want action and we want it now!"

"We want to know what you're going to do about these cougars."

"Get rid of them!"

Mr. Woods stood up calmly and addressed the crowd, "My team could remove the problem cougar within a day or two. If there is more than one cougar, as I suspect, it will take longer and cost more."

The mayor asked, "What do you mean by remove? Do you intend to catch it or kill it?"

"The current popular psychology is to relocate problem animals. If that's what you want me to do, I will. However, my experience with cougars tells me that relocation doesn't work. Did you ever hear of someone who got tired of a house cat, but didn't want to it put to sleep? So they drove ten miles away and let it out of the car. Two weeks later the same cat was back on their doorstep. My experience is that cougars are much the same. If we relocate your cougar, it'll probably be back. That's good for me, because I get paid twice, but it'll cost the city more to solve the problem. More importantly, you won't know when the cougar is back until you begin to have problems again. The decision is yours."

The mayor asked, "What do you charge to kill or remove the cougar?"

"The charge to kill one cougar is $25,000, to remove one is $30,000. If there's more than one, it'll be an additional $15,000 per cougar. I can draw up a contract tonight if you like. You only need to give me the go-ahead."

The city managers put their heads together, $25,000. They all agreed that was an outrageous amount of money. The budget couldn't allow that amount.

Sheriff Tate decided he'd better speak up now, since no one in the audience knew what he had just found out from the Skoko County Sheriff.

"Excuse me please, I have just taken a phone call from Sheriff Mitchell over in Skoko County. He found the body of Steven Long, a missing Newtown man, in the National Forest section near Cross Point today. The man had been killed and eaten by a cougar, probably on Sunday. In the process of looking for Steven Long one of his deputies was also killed. This afternoon the sheriff and four of his deputy's killed three cougars that were eating the deputy at the time."

Everyone in attendance just sat there, stunned. They all looked around at each other as each person digested the current news, many of them visibly paled. The mayor stood up.

"The potential for litigation against the city, if any one were to be killed, would be in the millions. In view of our fiduciary responsibility, I recommend we contract

Mr. Woods to kill the cougar." The council vote was unanimous.

The mayor stood up. "The job is yours Mr. Woods. We want you to kill it as soon as possible."

To the audience she said, "There will be no school throughout the city again tomorrow. Hopefully we'll have good news by tomorrow night. I recommend you keep your children and pets inside until we have solved this problem."

The audience was both relieved and grateful that the city managers had made the right decision. Get rid of the thing was the general consensus, and the sooner the better. You could hear it in their conversations as the audience started to disperse, anxious to get home.

"We don't feel safe going outside."

"Our children are not safe until the cougar is killed."

The Naturalist Club group was upset. One of the members nudged Sally.

"Aren't you going to get up and do something? They're going to kill the cougar!"

"I'm thinking, maybe a cougar in a residential area isn't a good idea."

"Are you nuts, they're going to kill the cougar. We have to stop them."

Sally turned to the member and asked, "Mr. Woods said the cougar would come back if they try to relocate it, what else can they do with it?"

"Put it in a zoo," the club member replied.

Sally thought it sounded like a reasonable idea. She quickly stood up and asked, "Why not capture the cougar and give it to a zoo?"

"That's a very logical thing to do and we'd be happy to if we could, but the zoos don't want them. They have plenty of cougars in the zoos around the country now and they are very expensive to keep. They eat a lot of meat every day, and it needs to be fresh, making it even more expensive."

"In some of the eastern states it's legal to have a cougar as a pet. The owners quickly learn when the kitten grows larger that it's very expensive to feed the big cat. The zoos won't take them so the owner just lets it loose. These animals can cause unique problems because they are accustomed to being around humans. They are comfortable being around humans and may take up home range near populated areas."

"What are the other alternatives, what can be done without killing it?"

Shaking his head Mr. Woods replied, "I'm not aware of any other solution that actually works. I wouldn't be too concerned. There's plenty of them out there right now. That's essentially why you're having problems. There's too many of them and there is no place else for them to go."

The mayor then added, "Not everyone in the city is here tonight, I'll have announcements made on the radio, local paper, and TV about the danger. Notify people to keep their children and pets inside, and that there's no school until we have the cougar. Please make sure your neighbors are aware of the danger in case they have not heard about it."

Photo by Lee Dygert

11

Mr. Woods and his two assistants went to work at four in the morning. They concentrated their efforts around the city maintenance yard. They had a license with the state to use dogs to hunt and eliminate predatory animals in populated areas. They also had the latest technology, which included infrared goggles.

The military developed the infrared technology years ago. Many things that are developed by the military research and development branches eventually end up in the civilian society. New technology and mass production manage to reduce the cost of the product to the point where things can be sold to the general public at a reasonable cost.

The infrared goggles allowed the team to work at night. They are sensitive to heat and present images of anything that radiates heat in the dark. The latest technology presents the image in color. Some of the better equipment could present an image with nearly the quality of a photograph taken in the daylight. This equipment would make it easy enough to identify a cougar at night. It's also useful in the daytime. It senses anything that radiates heat, so if a cougar was in a bushy area it could detect the heat differences.

Mr. Woods had a two-way radio set up to communicate with the Newtown Sheriff's on-duty deputy. They made arrangements to keep the Sheriff's office up to date on their position and progress.

"Newtown Sheriff, this is team leader, over."

"Team leader, this is Newtown Sheriff, go ahead," was the quick response.

"Newtown Sheriff, this is team leader, we are preparing to start the search from the city maintenance yard."

"Team leader, this is Newtown Sheriff, roger, keep us informed of any developments, out."

Trying to find cougar tracks would be hit and miss, mostly miss. The ground conditions had to be right; sand, mud or wet ground leave good tracks. Wherever the ground is covered with leaves, weeds, or grass it is much harder if not impossible to find the cougar's tracks. Cougar's paws are very big, hunters have reported them to be sometimes six to seven inches across. Actual measurements by scientists reveal a large print to be about four and a half inches by four and a half inches, but this is still much larger than a large dog's prints. The tracks are similar to a dog's track, except for some notable difference, dogs can't retract their claws so they leave the imprint of the claw with the footprint. Cats usually walk with the claws retracted. While the tracks look the same to the untrained, the cat's usually don't leave any claw marks.   There are exceptions to this.   If the cat is traversing rough terrain, slippery ground or going up hill. Under these circumstances using the claws helps them to get a better purchase on the ground. When they do use claws the imprint usually looks like a slash mark. As opposed to the claw imprint that dogs leave which usually looks like a dot at the leading edge of the toe pad.

Dogs are invaluable when tracking problem cougars because they sniff for the cat's scent. Once the dogs get the scent, they can follow the trail for long distances, regardless of the ground conditions.

They began the search behind the maintenance yard where the cougar had jumped the fence. It was a woodsy area, but not too dense. The three-dog team sniffed around from side to side along the fence line, quickly getting the scent, and the chase was on. The dogs led them through the woods for about twenty minutes. It was still dark so Mr. Woods led his men while wearing the infrared goggles. The dogs moved much faster than the men could travel in the dark. They went down a hill into a gully, and it was tough going for the team because it was so wet. They slipped and slid most of the way down the hill. By the time they reached the bottom of the gully they were all a muddy, sloppy mess. They continued to follow the sound of the dogs.

The dogs disappeared into an area of thick brush and blackberry bushes, following a game trail going into the brush. It was about twenty inches high and twenty inches wide and too thick for them to pursue. If the men were to follow the dogs they'd have to get down on their hands and knees to crawl through. Mr. Woods stopped to take a good look around the area with the infrared goggles. It was too dense to see into the brush without them, but he could see the blurred images of the three dogs moving around. There was another image in the bushes too, but he couldn't quite make out what it was.

"I don't like the look of this. Let's wait out here for a few minutes and see what happens with the dogs."

The juvenile cougar was lying in the thicket of blackberry bushes. She'd found a wide area inside the thicket where she had plenty of room and was out of the elements, dry and warm. It was a good place to pick off raccoons, rabbits, and possum as they traveled along the trail. It had been a safe place, until now. She grew agitated, as the baying dogs got closer. Suddenly, there was a dog in front of the cougar, blocking her exit. She let out a blood-curdling screech and swung a front claw into the dog, ripping a gash down its side. She stuck her claws back into the dog and flung it down the trail. The dog was wounded, but not severely. The cougar took off down the other side of the trail and was out in the open in less than five seconds.

One of the dogs let out a scream of pain, as all the dog's barking changed pitch to one of fervent pursuit. Mr. Woods was sweeping the whole area with his infrared goggles.

"There goes the cougar, up there!" he pointed.

They took off around the thicket, and one of the men turned on a high-powered flashlight. They caught a fast glimpse of the cougar running up the hill with the dogs coming out of the blackberry thicket in hot pursuit. The men headed up hill too, following the sound of the dogs. When they reached the crest of the hill, it was starting to get light and now they could see the dogs running out in the open.

The dogs split up, one directly behind the cat, one to the right side, and the other to the left. The dog behind the cat was gaining fast so the cat stopped and faced the dog directly behind it, fangs bared, ready to strike. The other dogs quickly came in from the sides, one coming in behind the cat. The cougar backed up to a small tree and sat down to protect its backside. The three dogs surrounded the cat staying at a safe distance, barking and growling at the cat.

When the three men came running up to the snarling group it was a stalemate for the animals. For the team, it was a successful hunt. This was one of two ways a cougar hunt with dogs usually ended for them, the cat would go up a tree or sit down with a tree behind it, to protect it's back side. Either way it's over for the cougar.

Mr. Woods took his nine-millimeter pistol out of his shoulder holster and dispatched the cougar with one shot. They waited about five minutes before approaching the dead cougar. They examined the cougar and determined it to be a female juvenile, about one hundred pounds. As he expected, it appeared to be about two years old. Considering what happened in the community over the past few weeks, this wasn't likely to be the same cougar that'd been causing problems on the other side of town. At this age it probably left its mother recently, maybe from a litter nearby, and was searching for an area of its own.

Mr. Woods dressed the wounds of the clawed dog. It's an occupational hazard for the dogs, but he knew this dog would fully recover in a week or two. Dog's wounds are not always this easy to resolve, he'd lost several good tracking dogs over the years on cougar and bear hunts.

He got his radio out and made the call. "Newtown Sheriff, this is team leader, over."

"Team leader, this is Newtown Sheriff, go ahead," came the response.

"Newtown Sheriff, this is team leader, we have just killed a cougar. It was a female juvenile, approximately one hundred pounds. We're on our way back to the maintenance yard now, over."

"Team leader, this is Newtown Sheriff, I understand you have killed a female cougar of approximately one-hundred pounds. What's your destination after you arrive at the maintenance yard?" The sheriff knew he should alert the mayor and other officials, knowing they will want to see it.

"Newtown Sheriff, this is team leader, we'll bring it over to the sheriff's office."

"Roger, what's your ETA, over?"

"I estimate we'll arrive at your office in about one hour."

They had about a mile or so to walk back to the maintenance yard. To make the carrying more manageable they tied the cougar's paws together and then broke off a branch from a dead tree, sliding the branch between the paws. The walk took about an hour. Once back they loaded the cougar into the back of the truck and drove to the sheriff's office. There was a large crowd of people when they arrived.

The mayor and the city council members looked at the cougar with awe. They couldn't believe the paws were so big and the legs so thick and powerful. The Sheriff and his deputies looked at the cat and were thankful they hadn't been required to go out looking for it, especially after what had happened in Skoko County this week.

Mr. Woods looked at the mayor and council, "I'm not convinced this is the only cougar you have in the city area. We'll go to the school area next and then to the other side of town if we don't find anything. We'll continue to search around the area until we can definitely determine whether or not this is the only one."

They went to Von Elementary School and radioed the sheriff and told them they were beginning the search at the school. After an hour there was no response from the dogs and they felt confident that no cougar was in the area.

"Newtown Sheriff, this is team leader, over."

"Team leader, this is Newtown Sheriff."

"Newtown Sheriff, this is team leader. We haven't had any response from the dogs here. We'll relocate and call in our plans, out."

Mr. Woods took the team to the other side of town and radioed the sheriff telling him they were beginning the search again. He gave him a street address, just in case some of the neighbors might become suspicious of strangers in the area. They began searching around a housing area that had a woodsy, natural area, an ideal place for a cougar to be living undetected. The dogs picked up a scent in about twenty minutes and the chase was on again.

"Newtown Sheriff, this is team leader, we have a scent and we're following a trail up the hill."

"Roger Team leader, understand you have a new pursuit, keep us informed."

"Roger, out."

The dogs were obviously following a scent, but they weren't running and baying. They were following it methodically, slowly, sniffing around to get the scent back again. It was a solid scent, but probably more than a day old. The dogs were working their way up the hill and away from the houses. The team continued to follow the dogs for two hours and they were about four miles away from the housing area. Still there was no visual sighting of a cougar and the dogs were moving slowly. It was getting late and the team had been on the move since four this morning. Everyone was tired and it wouldn't be long before dark. It would be a different story if the dogs were in hot pursuit. The adrenaline would be pumping then and the fatigue would be negated by the pursuit.

Mr. Woods stopped the team for a rest. "We're getting quite a way out from the housing area. Obviously a cougar was in the area, but it has left, perhaps in search of a better food supply. We'll call off the search for now and I'll speak with the city officials when we return to determine our plan of action."

"Newtown Sheriff, this is team leader, over"

"Team leader, this is Newtown Sheriff, go ahead."

"We have a cold trail and we're returning to our truck. See you in about an hour, out."

"Team leader, Newtown Sheriff, roger, out."

They called in the dogs, which was no small task. The dogs didn't like to give up on a hunt. But, even they were tired, and sensed there wasn't going to be any more hot action. They all headed back to the housing area and arrived just as it was getting dark. After getting all the gear packed away in the truck they went back to the sheriff's station. The sheriff, mayor, and two council members were waiting for the team to return along with a news van full of the latest satellite transmitting communications gear for live newscasts.

The syndicated news team had been hanging around all day, waiting to get more footage of the next cougar brought in for all to see. They made big press out of the dead cougar that was killed near the Newtown City maintenance yard earlier in the day. They waited, like vultures, for more footage to put on the evening news. It was now going to be more like the eleven o'clock news by the time it was all over.

Mr. Woods reported they found a definite scent near the housing area and followed the scent for about three to four miles into the mountains. He couldn't determine how old the trail was.

"The cougar may have left the area to look for deer or a better hunting area. It's hard to tell where it might be now."

The mayor interrupted Mr. Woods and asked, "Could the trail you were following this afternoon be from the same cougar you killed this morning?"

"It's possible that the scent was from the same cougar. It seems unlikely though."

The news teams were all over the place, getting shots of everyone from all angles. The cameraman came in close to get a good shot of Mr. Woods, but he pushed him away.

"Get out of my face."

There was no love lost between him and news people. They never got anything right. No matter what you tell them they cut and edit so it comes out however they want it to. They can take a film and edit it so that it comes out the opposite of what was actually said.

The mayor asked, "What should we do now?"

"I feel pretty confident the cougar has left the area, at least for now. We can continue to search, if that's what you want us to do. In order to continue the search, we'll charge a fee of five thousand dollars per day to cover our expenses, it's in our contract. Strictly based on my findings at this time, I don't really recommend that course of action. The cougar more than likely has traveled a long way away by now."

The mayor asked, "Can we assume that it's gone?"

Mr. Woods reassured the mayor, "I think it is for now, but it's hard to say for sure, or for how long it might stay away. At this point there are a lot of unknowns."

"What do you propose we do then?"

"I suggest you go back to life as usual, but I strongly recommend we come back in one week. If we find nothing we should come back again in two weeks and again at three weeks. This would give us time to determine if the cougar has returned to the area, without it being a surprise to you again. We charge five thousand dollars per day to come back and check out the area, plus the previously agreed upon fee if we find and kill another cougar."

The news team was getting everything on film, which, due to technology, was being recorded at the station. It was already being edited for transmission on the next news flash opportunity and, of course, the eleven o'clock news.

The mayor confidently stated, "That sounds like a good plan. I, and the community, would like to thank you and your team for your assistance in resolving this problem for us."

She looked into the camera and said, "Our cougar problem in Newtown is solved. We can all go back to life as usual and all schools will be back on schedule tomorrow with a normal routine."

Pulling the mayor aside, out of the view of the camera, Mr. Woods reiterated, "I'd like to stress my concerns about the likelihood there was a second cougar in the area. If I'm correct, there is a good chance it will return within the next few weeks."

Photo by Lee Dygert

12

Marie picked up the telephone. They'd just finished dinner and were cleaning up the table. It was Sally, their next-door neighbor.

"Did you hear they killed the cougar this morning? I just got the news from a friend. They're sure there are no more in the neighborhood and it's life back to normal. Can you believe it? They killed it, such a beautiful animal. I'm outraged! Why didn't they tranquilize it and move it out into the woods someplace? Why couldn't they give it to a zoo? Surely, there's a zoo somewhere that would take it. I'm ashamed of them for not even trying an alternative."

Marie was quick to say, "Well, I for one am glad the cougar isn't roaming around the neighborhood any more. Having a cougar in your backyard hardly seems safe to me, especially for the children. Thanks for the call Sally.

I appreciate you letting us know it's all over. Let's plan on dinner sometime. Talk to you later," and hung up.

Marie told Buck and the kids the good news.

"Great. What was that about getting together with them for dinner?"

"We need to go out more, get to know the neighbors, and make some new friends here. You know, I miss the old Navy squadron days, there was so much camaraderie. We had lots of friends, and we were always doing something together. There was a squadron function nearly every weekend. Maybe we should try a dinner with the Everhart's?"

"Yeah, I miss the camaraderie too, but I'm not interested in a friendship with the Everhart's. She's a tree hugger, she and her buddies put my dad and all his logger friends out of work. My dad would go through the roof if he knew we were hanging around with her, and Doug's an asshole." Buck wasn't one to sugar coat things.

"Buck, that's not a nice thing to say about a neighbor. Besides, the kids can hear you."

"Have you ever talked to him? Asshole is the correct description."

Buck opened the mail. They received a letter from the high school addressed 'to the parents of Eric Logan.' It was his grade report for the quarter and as usual, he received all A's and B's. Next he opened the letter addressed to the parents of Robert Logan. It was the same thing, all A's and B's. He proudly showed the letters to Marie and they agreed both the boys were doing great in school. They had started a family incentive when the kids were very young, Eric was in the third grade. The incentive was to encourage the children to get good grades in school. Every time they received all A's and B's on their report card, Buck would take them out of school for a day and take them skiing or go someplace special, if it wasn't ski season.

Buck and Marie got the boys together and told them their report cards had arrived. They both smiled a beaming smile and told them congratulations on receiving all A's and B's again. They were both doing great in school and they were very proud of their accomplishments. They explained that since ski season was over they wouldn't be able to take the day off from school to go skiing. Instead, Buck offered to take the boys fishing or play golf. Under the circumstances they wanted to take the day off no matter what, so they chose a fishing trip to Crystal Lake. They hadn't been there for about two years and it was a beautiful secluded lake. They wanted their reward as soon as possible, but tomorrow was Friday, so they decided to go on Monday. They went out to the garage and got all the fishing gear together and set aside for a quick get-away on Monday morning. This way they'd be at the lake early because fishing is usually better just as the sun is coming up, or close to it.

Sally was enraged. How could they condone killing such a beautiful animal. She called the president of the Naturalist Club and told him all the gory details. They decided to picket city hall the first thing Monday morning. He assured her that he would get their phone tree started. It was important to get the word out for a full-scale demonstration.

Sally sat down and wrote a letter to the mayor on behalf of the Naturalist Club. It condemned the city mayor and council members for supporting such an act of savage barbarianism. How could they hire someone and use public money to commit such an outrageous act against one of nature's most beautiful animals? The

Naturalist Club intended to sue the city. They wouldn't allow the city to kill the wild animals.

Photos by Lee Dygert

13

Monday morning Buck got up at five a.m. and woke the boys up. He went downstairs to the kitchen and got a pot of coffee going, then turned on the stove to heat the griddle. The pancakes were almost ready as Eric and Rob strolled into the kitchen.

"What's for breakfast?" asked Eric, trying to stifle a yawn.

Rob saw the pancake griddle was full of cakes. "Pancakes, my favorite."

"They'll be ready in a minute." He was making their lunches for a day of fishing at the lake. He put five sandwiches in the cooler and packed it to the top with a variety of snacks. He'd been on many day trips with his boys and knew they could eat a lot. Sometimes they'd bring friends along on fishing trips, and he wouldn't be able carry enough food for all of them.

After they all had their fill of pancakes they each rinsed off their plates and put them into the dishwasher.

Buck closed the dishwasher after putting his plate and silverware in and said. "Let's rock and roll! Time to go fishing."

The fishing gear was loaded in the van the night before, so they were ready to go by five-forty. He grabbed his small survival class pack and they headed out to the garage.

It was still dark as they drove up into the mountains. Crystal Lake was located approximately twenty-five miles away. They arrived in the parking area at six thirty and no other cars were there. Good, Buck thought, more fish for them. They took all of their gear out of the car, the cooler, fishing poles, bait, fish stringer, and his survival pack, which contained a raincoat for each of them. It wasn't raining, but in the northwest, it could at any time. Buck put on the pack, he'd planned it just right, and they were on their way just as the sun was coming up.

It was a little over a mile from the parking lot to the lake, and it was an easy hike. The light was peeking through the trees just enough light to see where they were going. The trail was in good shape, and well marked. It would be difficult to get off the trail by accident. By seven o'clock they could see the lake. When they arrived Buck chose to go to the north side, where there were some nice deep holes. Most people who went to the lake would go south, because it's more open and an easier trail.

Swawa, the cougar, was lying on a large branch, up against the tree trunk, about fifteen feet off the ground, lazily watching the three humans hike up the trail. She'd just arrived in the area yesterday, in search of her own territory. She'd killed and eaten a raccoon yesterday so she wasn't starving, but was ready for more food. Because she ate Steven Long and Deputy Moore, humans were now considered part of her diet, but three men together didn't present a realistic attack, still the possibilities were there if she was hungry enough.

Sally and over two dozen Naturalist Club members were ready to protest at Newton City Hall at seven forty-five. They all had pickets in hand which read; 'Fire the Mayor', 'Barbarians', 'Fire the City Council', 'No crimes against nature', 'Cougars are beautiful animals', 'Animal killers', etc. They were all chanting slogans.

"No more killing animals."

The mayor arrived just minutes before eight. The group of protesters immediately began to harass her.

"Fire the mayor! Cougar killer! Shame on you!" they yelled. She managed to get past them, going straight to her office she picked up the phone and dialed the Sheriff's personal number.

"Sheriff Tate here."

"Get over here and get these idiots out of here, " she yelled.

"What idiots?"

She calmed down a bit when she realized the sheriff had no idea what was going on.

"There's a group of protesters outside city hall protesting the killing of the cougar on Friday. Would you come over here and try to disperse them, please?"

"Sure thing," he assured the mayor.

The new shift was just beginning and roll call had been taken. Several deputies were walking out to their cars, but two stayed, hanging around the front desk. He waved them over.

"Come with me over to city hall, there's a bunch of protesters there."

To the desk sergeant he said, "Notify the others not to get too far away for now. We may need some assistance."

When Sheriff Tate arrived they were met with the same haranguing. He went up to the group leader and explained they were to keep it peaceful, not to damage anything or harass anyone. He wouldn't hesitate to arrest anyone who committed an unlawful act.

The group leader shouted into the sheriff's face. "You are the one responsible for killing the cougar! You are the one that should be arrested! You are the one that has committed the crime!" All the while jabbing his finger toward the sheriff's chest.

The sheriff's two brothers were loggers before a handful of tree huggers shut down the whole logging industry. The protesters where the same kind and there was no love lost here. Both of his brothers were unemployed for the last four years and having financial problems and marital problems because their wife's salary wasn't enough to support a family. Unemployed loggers were everywhere. They both went to the community college for over a year to learn new vocations. The state and the unemployment insurance department even had a special program to retrain the dislocated workers. It was to no avail, they're both over fifty now, and probably would never work again unless they go into business for themselves. No company would hire anyone that old in today's business environment.

One of the protesters hit the sheriff's car with a poster. The two deputies were on him in a flash. Pinned down, face on the parking lot pavement, and handcuffs on before he knew what hit him. As the other protesters watched, some decided it wasn't worth getting roughed up or arrested.

The sheriff looked over at the group with his hand on the butt of his revolver. "Anyone else want to go to jail?"

Two of the protesters spoke up, "Yes, but we'll go peacefully."

Sally was one of them, thinking this is great, just like old times, during the spotted owl protests. She almost smiled as she thought, this will surely get into the newspapers and on this evening's news. The more publicity we get, the better it is for our cause and all the more difficult it'll be for the city officials.

The deputies cuffed the two and put them into the car along with the first protester they'd arrested. Things began to calm down and the sheriff said to the leader. "Keep it peaceful."

Sheriff Tate grabbed the radio out of his car through the window and radioed the deputy on duty.

"Send two additional deputies over to city hall. We'll stay here till they arrive. I'm bringing in three protesters and I'll leave deputy Wade here with the two you're sending over." His gut feeling told him there wouldn't be any more problems, but he'd leave three deputies there just in case.

Buck and the boys found a deep, clear fishing hole that was big enough for the three of them to fish. The sun was coming up over the mountains as they made their first cast and Eric got a strike immediately, but it jumped out of the water and threw the hook. A hit on the first cast was a very good sign for a fisherman and they were all pumped up for a great day of fishing. It was looking like they picked a good site, at least for starters.

Crystal Lake supported a wide variety of trout. The usual rainbows, browns, cutthroat and brook trout, but also a few native dolly varden and an occasional kokanee or silver trout. The kokanee trout was a greenish blue with faint speckling, the sides and belly are silvery with no distinct spotting. They are delicious fish, but hard to catch. First, there aren't a lot of them, and second, they have thin tissue around the jaw. Frequently, the kokanee is caught in the jaw area near the hinge of the upper and lower jaw. Since the tissue is weak the hook has a tendency to pull through during the fight to land it and the fish gets away.

By eleven thirty Eric and Rob each landed three nice trout. Eric caught two rainbows and a cutthroat while Rob's were a cutthroat, a dolly varden, and a brown. Buck had plenty of fish on the line, but only landed one, a twenty-two inch brown. He went for quality, not quantity. His was easily the largest of the day's catch, so far.

"Anybody getting hungry? "

"Always!" Eric and Rob replied in unison.

They decided to take a break for lunch and Buck opened the cooler, handing out the food and drinks. The day was beautiful, not too warm, about fifty degrees, but the sun was out. In the northwest, any time the sun is out, it's a bonus day. Rob was pointing excitedly at the sky.

"Look, a bald eagle is circling above us."

Buck and Eric looked up and sure enough, a bald eagle was circling fifty feet above them, intently looking for a meal. Eagles and osprey are fairly common in the northwest. It's mesmerizing to watch them, such a beautiful and graceful bird. They soar for hours and barely flap their wings, riding the air currents. When they did flap their wings you can get a better feeling for the size of the bird, they're very big birds. The eagle tucked its wings in and went into a dive. About five feet off the water, right in front of them, the eagle spread its wings, reaching out with its claws and plucked a nice fat trout from the water. There were four ducks sitting in the water about twenty feet from where it grabbed the fish. They saw it coming and scattered to the wind, not wanting to be it's next meal.

The sun felt great and they all stretched out to enjoy those beams of warmth. Eric asked. "How come people get divorced?" He just found out that his best friend's parents were getting a divorce. All three of the children had mentioned, from time to time in the past year, that many of the kids they knew at school only had one parent.

Buck answered, "Life can be complicated, as you'll find out someday. People change as they grow older. Most divorces are caused by one of four things, sex, money, a combination of two, or more recently abuse. Usually the problem is sex and money"

"I don't get it," said Eric.

"Sexual incompatibility can be a major factor. Sex is a strong driving factor in life and in a marriage."

"The second reason that many marriages fail is money. No matter how much money you make, it's never enough, and very few people understand how to manage money. People seem to want everything, and they want it right now. They buy whatever they want and put it on a credit card and the debt just keeps growing to the point where it can't possibly be paid off. Sometimes, one of the couple will realize that this can't go on, but the other continues to spend more than they have."

"When it comes to managing money, you have to pay yourself first. By that I mean, put a certain amount of money into the bank every time you get paid, and just leave it there. It's for major life purchases, emergencies, and retirement. The amount depends on where you are in your life. If you are single, maybe as much as thirty per cent, depending on how much you make. Once you are married, it depends on whether you have two wage earners or one. With a two-income household you might be able to save the entire earnings of one person's salary, that'd be the ideal situation. After you have children, the amount you can save will decrease, especially as they get older. The critical point is that you put the money in the bank every time you get paid and live on what's left. If you want something and you don't have the extra cash to pay for it, you can't have it, it's as simple as that. Never borrow money to pay for anything except a house. Everything else you must have the discipline to save until you have cash to pay for it. When you start getting into debt and it grows every month, there'll be a lot of arguments around the house."

"People change as they grow older too and you have to change together. Find a woman that likes to do the same kind of things you like to do, and change together."

"When you are ready to get married, take a good look at her mother. Your girlfriend will probably have similar personality traits and look like the mother in twenty years. If her mother is overweight and the house is a dirty mess, it's most likely the way your girlfriend will be in about twenty years."

"Disagreements on how to raise children can be a source of marital disharmony too. Men tend to be strict about discipline and women tend to be the opposite. You've got to find a happy medium that works for everyone."

"In the end analysis, it's usually a problem that's related to sex and/or money."

The clouds were on their way back and it started to mist. The change in weather got the fish to jumping and they scrambled to their poles to get in to the action. Around four o'clock Buck noticed that Eric wasn't there.

"Where'd Eric go?"

"He's taking a leak."

"I don't remember him leaving. How long ago did he take off?"

"Oh, maybe fifteen or twenty minutes ago."

"That seems like quite a while for a leak."

"Maybe he had a hard time finding the right tree," Rob said chuckling.

Eric walked out into the woods to relieve himself. He didn't really need to go far, but it was easy walking and the fish had stopped biting so there was no hurry. He figured he might as well explore a little. He stopped when he found a good spot and as he stood there peeing he caught a foul stench. He thought, 'I don't remember farting in the last few minutes, maybe there's something dead around here.' Hearing the bushes move, he turned to look toward the noise, and out came a big black bear about twenty feet away.

"Holy crap!" he cried out, and took off running.

He ran down the trail with the bear in hot pursuit. After several minutes he came to a ravine about twenty feet deep with lots of fallen trees lying across it, there was nowhere else to go. Jumping onto one of the trees that made a bridge over the stream he started across. When he was about half way, the tree broke loose from the far bank, rolled, and threw Eric off. He landed in the stream at the bottom with a painful crack as the log fell too. The stream was from snow runoff and was very cold with the temperature somewhere around forty degrees Fahrenheit. When the log fell it rolled to a stop across Eric's legs, just above the knees. He couldn't budge the tree, and his legs were in excruciating pain. He wished he were back in school now.

The good news was the bear apparently lost interest, because it was nowhere in sight.

"Help!" He suddenly realized he was too far away for Dad or Rob to hear him. He thought, 'I'm in real trouble here.' He remembered one of his teachers telling him about E.S.P (extra sensory perception) and telepathy, ways of sending messages from one person to another via brain waves. He began to concentrate.

"Dad, I need help," over and over again in his head.

Buck felt an impulse that something was wrong with Eric, it was like an electric shock. He'd been gone too long. "I'm going to look around for Eric, Rob. You stay here in case he comes back."

Buck went into the woods calling for Eric. After ten minutes and no response, he went back to Rob. "Come on Rob, we need to go search for Eric. It's almost four thirty. It'll be dark before long and we need to be back to the car before it gets nightfall."

Buck grabbed his pack and put it on as they went into the woods to look for Eric. They walked around together calling "Eric" every few minutes.

Rob said, "Let's split up and look for him."

"No, it's getting late. We only have about an hour before it starts getting dark. I don't want all of us to be lost."

He thought, what would you tell your outdoor education students to do in a situation like this? Use the whistle! In his classes he always told the students to carry a whistle, like the one that coaches use at games. It doesn't take much energy to use, but it produces a loud sound that's unlike any natural sound you will hear in the woods.   Anyone hearing it will know right away the sound is connected to a person. He dug around through his pack until he found the whistle and gave it to Rob.

"Blow it every twenty to thirty seconds, one short sharp blow."

Each time Rob blew the whistle Buck listened intently, as they continued to walk north on the trail. Buck thought he heard or felt something, it was like a magnetic pull, drawing him in one direction. Rob kept blowing the whistle every thirty seconds and suddenly, they both heard it.

"DAD!"

The sound drew them toward the ravine and when they reached the edge they looked over and saw Eric under the fallen tree. They scrambled down the side to the streambed where Eric laid, pale and cold, but conscious. He'd been lying in the cold water too long, Buck thought and hypothermia would set in soon if we don't get him out of the water fast.

Buck and Rob tried to pick up the tree to free Eric, but they couldn't budge it. Stepping back Buck looked around to evaluate the situation. He remained calm so that Rob wouldn't panic. This is a life-threatening situation that could leave them helpless to liberate Eric.

"We need to get something to use as a fulcrum so we can move the tree that's trapping him."

Trying to reassure Eric, Buck told Eric, "Hang on, we'll get you out of here."

Eric only moaned. He was so weak he could barely speak. Shivering he said, "Dad, I'm so cold and my leg hurts real bad."

Searching the streambed Buck saw plenty of deadfall laying all over.

"Come on Rob, help me move this one."

They grabbed a log that was about twenty feet long and six inches in diameter, wedging it under the log and pushing up. The log broke under the pressure, probably too old and beginning to decay. They needed to find a newer fallen tree. They quickly began looking for another until they found a good one. Buck re-evaluated the situation. It was beginning to get dark and it was now raining, normal for the northwest, but not good right now because the stream was slowly rising. Soon the water would be over Eric's head. They had to get the log off Eric fast, because he was now shaking from the cold, a sign that he may go into shock. This time they placed the fulcrum log farther up the bank. It would require less movement at the business end, providing it didn't break again. Buck went over to Eric, he was barely conscious now.

"Eric, we're going to try to move the log again. When we push the tree up, try to roll over to your right to get out from under it."

"OK," but it came out weak.

The situation had turned into a life or death situation too fast. They had to make it work, time was running out as the stream continued to rise. Buck and Rob pushed up on the log for all they were worth. The tree only moved slightly, but it looked like it was enough for Eric to get free.

"Eric, roll out," but Eric didn't move.

Buck moved up the bank and strained to put the log under his shoulder and move up some more, lifting the tree slightly more off of Eric, the pain was excruciating. He was holding up five hundred pounds of tree.

Buck managed to say to Rob, "Go over and pull him free."

Rob quickly ran over to his brother and dragged him out from under the tree, finally freeing him. As soon as

Buck could see that Eric was free, he eased his grip on the log, but he slipped and it threw him into the stream. He was soaking wet anyway from trying to free Eric in the stream and from the rain. He lay there for a moment exhausted, but relieved as Rob tried talking to Eric.

Eric was unconscious, passed out from the pain and the cold water and now it was getting darker. All three were soaking wet and as the sun went down the temperature began dropping fast. What seemed like a simple day of fishing this morning turned into a life or death survival situation that could happen to anyone. If you are prepared, your chances of survival are much better.

Buck and Rob carried Eric up out of the ravine and sat down to rest on the bank and think about their situation.

"Eric is in serious trouble Rob. He has hypothermia and we've got to get him warmed up fast or he could die."

Buck looked around. It was dark and hard to see much, but he found a huge fallen tree with a large stump at one end, just what he was looking for. It was the best they could hope for at this point. Buck instructed Rob to find some loose branches and lay them against the big tree, creating a makeshift shelter, and then he started taking off Eric's clothes.

Marie was accustomed to her guys being late when they were fishing. During fishing trips the boys completely lost track of time. It was unimportant, especially when they were catching fish. However, it was now after ten o'clock and she hadn't heard from them yet. If they were fishing at the shore it'd be no big deal, but they were at the mountain lake today. She was getting concerned because Buck said they should be home around six, which could easily mean seven or eight, but not ten without him contacting her. When they're fishing they're in a time warp, if the fish are really biting they might stay forever in some places, but not at Crystal Lake. They have to hike in and Buck would never attempt to make the hike in the dark, it's too dangerous. He always tells his survival classes never travel in the forest when it's dark. The chances of getting hurt or even worse, are too high. At first she thought maybe they stopped on the way home for something to eat, but Buck always took plenty of food. There was no place to eat between the lake and Newtown, if they were in Newtown he would have called by now. Plus, tomorrow was a school day and Buck would not have kept them out this late. Something had to be wrong.

Marie called the Newtown sheriff and told the duty deputy the situation. There are children involved and their safety is paramount. The deputy took her information and told her he would check it out. He quickly determined that Crystal Lake was in the jurisdiction of the Skoko County Sheriff's Department. He called them and relayed the story, asking them to check it out.

The Skoko County sheriff sent a deputy up to the Crystal Lake area to check it out. When the deputy arrived she found one car matching the Logan's license and vehicle type provided by the Newtown Sheriff's Department. Everything looked normal and there was no sign of forced entry or foul play, but it was dark and in a very secluded place. In view of the fact that only a few days ago deputy Moore and the jogger were killed and eaten by cougars, the whole sheriff's department was on edge. She was especially aware of the danger being out in the woods at night by herself.

She yelled, "Mr. Logan," a few times. When there was no response, she called in to report her findings and recommended a search be initiated. The deputy notified the Newtown Sheriff's Department of their findings and told them they were initiating a search party and they would keep them informed of their progress.

When Buck got Eric's clothes off he began taking off his own clothes. Rob thought he'd gone nuts.

"Ah Dad, what're you doing?"

"Eric has hypothermia, we've got to get him warmed up fast. I'm going to transfer my body heat to him to warm him up. Under the circumstances, it's the only way to warm up a person with hypothermia."

Buck took a raincoat and a tarp out of his pack and lay down naked next to Eric, wrapping him up in the raincoat. Rob lay down on the other side, with Eric sandwiched between the two of them. They pulled the raincoat in tight to keep all the heat in. Buck rubbed Eric's arms to create heat from friction. It seemed like forever, but after about fifteen minutes, Eric started to move and after another ten minutes he was talking.

"I'm so cold."

Buck put their clothes back on. They were wet and cold, but fortunately, they all wore their new microfiber pullovers with hoods. The new fiber is much like wool, but more comfortable and will keep you warm even when wet.

"Hang in there pal, you'll be OK."

Buck put a raincoat on Eric and covered them with a tarp to help preserve body heat since they were still out in the rain.

"Rob, can you go back to building a lean-to over the fallen tree so we can get Eric out of the rain? I'll stay here with Eric to keep him warm a little longer."

Rob went back to work building a lean-to shelter against the big deadfall tree. He found small logs and big branches and propped them up against the tree. He took another blue tarp out of the backpack and placed it over the shelter and put some more logs and branches over the edges to hold it securely and seal it tightly. The shelter was big enough for the three of them to sit down or lay down inside with enough room for a fire, if they could get one going.

Eric was moving around more and seemed to be out of the emergency stage of hypothermia, but now his leg was causing him a lot of pain. Buck took a close look at it and determined that it was broken. Most likely it was caused by the fall or else when the tree fell on him.

Buck sat with his back against the log, he needed to think about all this. First, it was clear to him they would have to spend the night there. Survival rule number one, never travel in the woods at night. In the desert, that was a different story, but they weren't in the desert. Next, they needed to prevent hypothermia and under the circumstances that meant a shelter. He thought about the first aid rules, if you have an injured person, check breathing, check bleeding, check for shock. It appeared they had solved the immediate hypothermia problem, at least for now, but with a broken leg, the pain and cold, he could go into shock from his injury.

"Rob, help me get Eric into the shelter. Be careful with his leg."

They dragged Eric into the lean-to shelter as he moaned and groaned the whole way. It was better inside, no rain, and it was more protective. Buck searched through his pack and found the small bottle he always kept for emergencies, which contained Tylenol and Benadryl. He gave Eric a Tylenol and a water bottle to help relieve the pain, telling him to drink plenty of water.

It would also make him more comfortable and relaxed. Eric was holding up pretty good considering the chain of events.

Together Buck and Rob set out to collect branches. Rob took to the task with great fervor, he was scared something might happen to his brother if they couldn't keep him warm and dry. He started breaking and cutting up pine branches. Together they laid more branches over the plastic tarp on the logs that were used to make the lean-to. When it appeared to be sufficiently covered they started laying branches on the floor inside of the shelter. This was to create an air barrier between the ground and the body. If you lay down or sit down on the cold ground it will suck your body heat out like a vacuum. Anything that can be used to make an air space between the ground and the body will help to preserve body heat.

Next they gathered moss and as many pine cones as they could find in the dark. The moss was put on the floor inside the shelter, it would soften their bed on the hard ground, mainly for comfort and the pinecones were for the fire. Buck took the other tarp and laid it over the branches on the floor inside the shelter. There was enough overlap to use as a blanket. Rob crawled inside the shelter and Buck added a few more logs outside before he crawled in. As he crawled inside he pulled a log in behind him to seal off the entryway. It was dark inside and they were all cold.

Buck cleared an area by the entrance, so he could make a fire inside the shelter. His hand searched through his survival pack in the dark until he found a butane lighter though. He flicked it, again and again, but it wouldn't light because his hands were wet. Damn, it wasn't going to work. He put his hand back into the backpack and continued to feel around the objects until he found what he was searching for; the steel wool, the metal match, and two small votive candles. He tore off a section of the steel wool and fluffed it up. Getting out his pocketknife he took the metal match and shaved off some pieces of the magnesium into the steel wool. He handed the two candles to Rob.

"Get ready to light these when I get the wool going."

He then placed the butt of the metal match against a chunk of wood with the steel wool right next to it and struck the flint with the blade of the knife. A spark flew from the flint into the steel wool and started to sparkle. Buck blew on the steel wool and it ignited into a brilliant flame.

In unison, Eric and Rob said, "Oh yes."

Rob managed to light both candles before the instantaneous bonfire quickly died out. Buck picked up two pinecones and gave one to Rob. Together they held them above the candle flames to dry them out, the pitch on the cones rapidly catching fire. They dropped the burning cones in the clear spot Buck had made earlier and began to build a fire. They kept repeating the process until they got a small fire going. When Buck was certain the fire wouldn't go out he blew out the candles to save them in case they were needed later. Now they all felt safe and comfortable, amazing what a little fire would do psychologically, but the heat it produced soon warmed up their humble abode.

It finally hit Rob, "We're not staying here are we? There's no television." Everyone chuckled, easing the tension their harrowing adventure had caused.

The shelter was successful in keeping out the rain, and the heat from the fire in such a small space, would quickly dry them out if they could keep it going. Buck realized their fire time might be limited and decided to make the best of the time they had left. The fire gave them enough light to get the inside organized so they improved the bed of pine branches on the ground to make it more comfortable and warmer. Rob got his pocketknife out and started to shave wood off the huge fallen log inside their shelter, carefully putting the shavings on the fire. Buck took four branches, about one to two inches in diameter and made a splint for Eric's leg with the rope he carried in his pack. Everyone laid down close together and he got the trash bags out and wrapped around them to seal in the heat from their bodies. Rob kept feeding the shavings to the fire to keep it going as long as possible. The coals would still provide some heat for a while after the fire went out, because they were running out of pinecones. Rob kept using his knife to get more shavings to feed the fire until he fell asleep from exhaustion.

Eric seemed unusually quiet so Buck checked him and he seemed a little warm. He searched around in his pockets until he found the bottle of pills and took out another Tylenol to give to Eric. He remembered he had two pairs of micro fiber gloves, one in the fishing vest and one in his pullover. He got them out and put them on each of his sons. They were small, light and thin, but every bit would help keep the boys warm. The fire warmed it up substantially inside the shelter, and they were beginning to dry out.

Shortly after midnight something moving around outside woke them up, hearing a hissing sound. Rob whispered, "What was that?"

Buck whispered back, "Shush, sounds like a cougar. Don't move or make any noise." They could hear the cougar sniffing around outside the shelter.

Swawa instinctively knew something was inside. She had been in the area long enough to know that something was different. She could smell the smoke from inside and sensed movement. She wasn't quite sure what it was, but she felt it was possibly prey. She put her paw against one of the logs, pushing, and clawing at it.

Inside they could hear the cougar's claws moving down the grain of the wood. Holding both of his sons in his arms, Buck tried to calm their nerves. Relax, he thought, animals can sense fear, if you relax they won't be able to sense your fear. They were so close they could have touched the cougar, through the tarp and logs. The cougar definitely felt their presence and she knew it was prey, she could smell them and their fear. She made a sharp hissing noise, trying to scare them into fleeing from their shelter.

Buck was proactive, not one to leave things to chance or luck. He'd never owned a handgun, much less carried one, even in the woods. The only time he'd ever carried a handgun was in the Navy, flying in the close proximity of hostile territory, but he wished he had one right now. Ever so slowly, and quietly, he got his survival bag and began searching through it in the dim light provided by the fire. His hand knew everything it touched and he finally found it, that familiar feel of his old Navy survival knife. The very same knife that he'd carried with him on over four thousand hours of flying missions. It wasn't much of a defense against a cougar, but he only had to get one good thrust in the right place.

It's three against one, actually two against the cougar, Eric wouldn't be much help in his condition. The broken leg made it hard for him to even roll over. It was dark, they were out of their element, and the cougar had the advantage.

Suddenly, there was a deafening roar, so loud the sound vibrated throughout the shelter, like thunder. Buck and the boys weren't sure what to think, this was a new twist to the drama that was unfolding in the darkness surrounding them.

The cougar spun around as the black bear attacked. The bear didn't like any other predator in its territory and he was much larger than the cougar. He hit the cougar at full speed and swung his massive paw, sending the cougar ten feet into the woods. She had three superficial claw wounds on her left forequarter as the bear attacked again, hitting her from behind and sending her into another cartwheel. She recovered quickly and went into the attack mode herself.

The bear weighed over three hundred pounds, the cougar weighed about one hundred pounds. The outcome seemed like a foregone conclusion. The bear is big, strong, and a fierce competitor in battle. Mountain men over the years have witnessed battles between bears and cougars and experience told them the battle could go either way. The cougar is fast, agile, smarter, and pound for pound, in some ways, much stronger than the bear.

The cougar bounded toward the bear, angled off, sprung ten feet up the trunk of a spruce tree, and jumped onto the back of the bear. She sank her claws into the bear's back and her teeth into the back of the bear's neck. Rolling over, the bear tried to dislodge the cougar, but the cat hung on and sunk her claws in deeper. She began raking her razor sharp rear claws down the bear's back with her powerful hind legs. The bear's hide was thick and the hair dense and matted, but her claws went right through it all, ripping big gashes down its back. The cat was wounded and enraged. She ripped and twisted her jaws, sinking her canine teeth deep into the bear's neck. Her front claws were deeply imbedded as she continued to rake her rear claws with ruthless abandon severing muscle and tendons. The ferocious attack was causing the bear to bleed profusely.

Bears are hard to kill and hunters going after bears know there are only two places that a single shot, from a high-powered rifle, will kill. The vital organs are well protected and the brain is very small. A bear that is shot can go a long way before it bleeds to death if not shot in a vital organ. A wounded bear has a nasty disposition, and attacks can be particularly brutal.

The bear couldn't get the cougar off its back and the battle went on for about twenty minutes while Buck and the boys laid in the shelter, only a few feet away, listening. The noise from the fight was awesome, roaring, growling, and screaming from both of the animals. They could hear them rolling around, swinging and gouging each other. Suddenly, it was over and the noise stopped, there was no more fighting. The next thing they heard was a ripping, tearing sound, they could hear teeth grinding against bone, gnawing, then slurping, and licking. One has killed the other and was eating it, only ten feet away from their shelter. The three of them lay there, very still, listening intently.

Eric was not feeling too great, with the broken leg and all, but he thought he remembered fishing trips being more fun than this. He whispered, "I don't know what I did to get here into this mess, but I swear I won't do it again."

They listened to the animal eating its victim throughout the night, glad it was out there and not in here with them. Buck guessed, from the sounds he heard, the cougar won the battle. He figured it would get plenty to eat and be gone by morning. The threat to them was all but eliminated, but it wasn't likely the boys would want to go fishing at Crystal Lake again anytime soon.

When the sun came up all was quiet, but no one was anxious to leave the safety of the shelter to get a better look outside. Buck place some twigs on the burning embers to get the fire going again. It was light enough to see inside the shelter now and Buck checked Eric's forehead again, it felt hot, plus his leg was swollen. Buck got another Tylenol and gave it to him along with some water to wash it down. He had immobilized the leg with a makeshift splint, but he hadn't been able to set it under the circumstances.   The mending process would have already started. Once they got him to the hospital they would need to break it and re-set it. Considering the way the day evolved, it would be better than some of the other possible alternatives.   Buck was sure a search party would be on the way near sunrise and it should be only a matter of hours before they were found.

The Mountain Rescue Team gathered at the Crystal Lake parking lot at five a.m. with the sheriff's deputy there to assist the team in whatever way she could. The rescue team had all the gear they might need for virtually any kind of rescue. Each member had a radio headset that was voice activated when it's in the active mode. They took off at first light and when they arrived at the lake the teams split up, one team going south, the other going north.   Within ten minutes the north team found the fishing poles and the stringer of fish. Actually, what was left of the fish, the raccoons had pretty much cleaned the stringer overnight. They notified the south search team and they all rendezvoused to begin the search in the woods from there.

Buck and Marie had been married for over twenty years. All the Navy training had taught them to think alike, both knowing what to do when a problem such as this presented itself. Buck anticipated Marie would call the sheriff and a rescue team would be looking for them soon after the sun came up.

Buck fished through his survival pack and found his infamous coach's whistle. It made a sound like no other sound in nature. The sun was up, and he was ready to be rescued. They hadn't heard anything outside the shelter for about an hour and he figured the victor must have left the area, at least for the time being. It would be back for more to eat later, but for now it seemed safe. He pushed the entryway log off to the side and looked around. All was quiet, so he worked his way out of the shelter and searched for signs of danger.

The bear lay there on the bank of the ravine, partly eaten.

"Looks like the cougar won the battle," Buck observed. The bear's internal organs had been removed and were in a neat pile about three feet from the dead bear. The back had long claw marks and the upper hind legs showed signs of deep wounds from the cougar's back legs pumping away during the battle. This caused bleeding which helped weaken the bear. Buck thought, it's amazing how the cougar can rip through that tough skin, the claws must be really sharp. He examined the bear carcass more closely studying the opened chest cavity. All of the internal organs were missing. He looked at the pile of intestines and quickly noted that the heart, lungs and liver were not there. He concluded that the cougar must have eaten them. The heart, lungs and liver on an animal this size must weigh about twenty to thirty pounds. It did not appear that the animal had eaten anything else, however twenty to thirty pounds at one feeding was quite a meal.

Considering the chain of events, trying to find Eric, Buck wasn't sure which way it was back to the lake, only that it was sort of south. He pointed the whistle to the south and gave it a long hard blow, bringing Rob out of the shelter.

Buck suggested, "Hey Rob, let's see if we can get a fire going out here."

It had stopped raining, temporarily, so Rob went to find some more pinecones. Buck's hands were cold, but dry and he took the butane lighter out of the pack and got a pinecone lit. Rob got some more going while Buck took his survival knife and shaved off pieces of wood from an old dead branch. Gradually, they added small pieces of wood until they had a good fire going. Then they helped Eric out of the shelter and put him close to the fire.

Relieved, Eric said, "Oh man, that really feels good."

He made it through the night like a trooper, hardly a complaint about the pain he must have felt and the cold surely made it worse. They were all very cold, but the fire was changing that now.

Rob took up the whistle duty so Buck could take a better look at Eric's leg. He was lucky it wasn't a compound fracture, which would be much worse and more likely to cause shock. An open, bleeding wound would've added to the difficulties of the night.

The rescue team started working their way north from where they had found the fishing poles. One of them thought he heard something, it sounded like a whistle. They all stopped to listen. Excited, they realized it was a whistle, knowing the father and sons were near. They headed off in the direction of the sound, but in the woods sound bounces off the trees, making the direction of the sound deceptive. Generally, there'd be about a thirty-degree range of accuracy following the sound.

Eric sat by the fire, his injured leg stretched out straight, the palms of his hands held out toward the fire.

"How are you doing Eric?" Buck inquired.

"I'm okay, my leg hurts quite a bit, but the heat from the fire feels really good."

"I feel pretty sure that mom will have called for help when we didn't return home last night. I'm confident that a rescue team will be out looking for us. I imagine they'll be arriving soon."

Buck cut off a big chunk of flesh from the dead bear's thigh and stabbed it onto a big stick and held it over the fire. They could now hear the rescue team coming through the woods, it wouldn't be long before they were found. Rob kept blowing the whistle about every ten seconds. Cooking bear meat has a very distinctive odor and the rescue team homed in on the smell. When they arrived, Buck was holding the stick over the fire.

"Breakfast is almost ready, hope you brought some hot coffee. I sure could use a steaming hot cup right now."

They looked at the bear in disbelief.

"Did you kill that bear?" one of the rescuers asked.

"A night in the woods can make a man hungry. The breakfast is compliments of a cougar that dropped by last night. It was quite a battle. We didn't get to watch it, but we sure heard it."

"That must have been a hair raising experience, so close to a cougar and a bear fighting to the death," one of the rescuer's said.

"It definitely had our full attention that's for sure," Buck replied. "It was real neighborly of him to leave us some breakfast though. Care for a bite? It's mighty tasty."

They all declined.

Buck stood up and offered his hand to one of the rescuer's. "Hi, I'm Buck, this is Eric, I'm pretty sure he has a broken leg. Rob and I are OK, but we could use some help getting Eric out of here."

They removed the makeshift splint that Buck put on the night before and confirmed the likely broken leg. They put a another splint on Eric's leg and made a stretcher out of two sturdy branches and some rope they had with them making it easier to carry Eric out.

The team leader used the radio to call in a report they'd found all three of them. He reported Eric's probable broken leg and that they would take all three to the hospital in Newtown for examination.

Swawa lay in the same tree as yesterday watching the rescue team carry Eric up the trail, watching with curiosity as they passed beneath her. She was tired, but full, and not really interested in moving. Later tonight she'd go back to the dead bear and feed again. She lay there licking her wounds as the men continued up the hill.

Buck was relieved when they got back to the parking area, they all were. Buck was especially thankful for all the survival training he had in the Navy. It turned out to be a life-saving and educational experience for him and his two sons.

The sheriff's office notified Marie that her husband and two sons had been found and were in good condition, except for Eric's broken leg. Marie and Wendy were waiting for them at the Newtown Hospital when they all arrived, they were obviously relieved to see them. Marie quickly determined for herself that they were all OK, in spite of Eric's injury. She gave each one of them a big hug.

Wendy asked, "Where's the fish?"

Photo by Lee Dygert

14

Marie decided she and Wendy would take the day off from work and school after their harrowing experience with the boys the day before. They both got up late, around ten o'clock, careful not to make any noise that might wake the boys up. All the guys at the Logan house were sleeping in. The girls were both happy that everyone was home safe and sound, the past two days were hard on them too.

"Let's get out of here and let them sleep. We'll go to the mall and get some Easter decorations and then we can go out to lunch."

"Oh good, I like going out to lunch with you Mommy."

Marie made a quiet check on each of her boys to reassure herself they were still there. They were all very lucky and she felt relieved. She left them a note letting Buck know their plans and they were off for a mother and daughter day.

Frank went out into the front yard early in the morning, hoping his cat would be out there waiting for him. Disappointingly, there was no sign of his 'Fluffy'. He went around to the backyard and into the shed where he stored his lawn mower and all his yard tools. He took his garden stool and the bucket of little garden tools over to the flowerbed behind the house and sat on the stool. He took the little rake out and began pulling it through the dirt to loosen the weeds. The azalea plant was just beginning to blossom, his wife had loved the azaleas. Of all the flowers in the garden they were her favorite. She liked them even better than the rhododendrons that were so beautiful. She passed on from breast cancer five years ago and he was still lost and lonely without her. Now his only companion, Fluffy, had disappeared.

He sat with his back to the woods pulling at the weeds. Behind the house his neighbors couldn't see him. He enjoyed listening to the bird's cheerful song as he worked in the yard and he could feel his loneliness fade a little. It was such a beautiful day.

Suddenly, he heard a loud hiss. His flesh got goose bumps and he looked around, but didn't see anything. He'd heard that noise before on television, perhaps the animal channel. Probably those damn kids trying to play another trick on him.

Frank gave up watching the news years ago. It was always the same depressing news, night after night. He didn't take a newspaper either, it was the same bad news all the time, and newspapers are too expensive. He was a loner, he rarely saw the neighbors, and Buck was about the only one he ever spoke to. Frank didn't have a clue there had been a cougar in the neighborhood. He probably wouldn't have done anything different anyway. He would have said, 'I'm almost eighty years old, what do I care.'

He got up slowly, stretching his crotchety old bones. The arthritis in his knees hurt when he was down picking weeds too long. He started around the side of the house and stopped to pick up a soda can. 'Damn kids,' he thought, 'I wish they'd stay out of my yard. They make a mess and make too much noise.' He went to the front yard and turned on the sprinkler and returned to the backyard again and resumed picking the weeds. He heard that same hissing sound again. 'Burr', he thought, 'all of a sudden it's cold.'

Frank sometimes lost track of time. He'd been picking weeds for quite awhile and his knees were beginning to hurt too much. He suddenly remembered he intended to mow the lawn today. Sometimes he was forgetful and got side tracked easy. He took the stool and tool bucket back to the shed and got the lawn mower out. After he fueled it up and checked the oil he gave it a crank. He had given up on the rope starter years ago and had his old mower equipped with a battery starter. He tried to get someone to mow the lawn for him years ago, but they wanted a small fortune to mow the lawn. Even the neighborhood kids want too much and they are so unreliable. They'd only mow it when they felt like it or needed money, so he kept mowing it himself, just a little slower each year. After two hours of slowly following the mower back and forth across the backyard he was bushed. It was getting late and he didn't have time or energy to do the front yard today, but it could wait until tomorrow.   He pushed the mower across the yard wobbling from side to side from fatigue. He sat down on a camp chair he kept next to the shed. He needed to rest before he put it all away.

The birds were filling the air with their spring song and the sun would soon begin to fade for the day. He'd accomplished quite a bit for one day. Then he heard it, or thought he heard it. It'd been a long day for Frank, and he was really tired, too tired. A meow.

"Fluffy?"

He got up and looked out into the woods.

"Fluffy, is that you?"

He went into the woods, trying to go where he thought he heard the meow.

"Fluffy." He went deeper and deeper into the woods, all he wanted was his companion back. After looking around for about ten minutes he saw it, a cat's tail and a paw. That was all, just the bloody tail and the paw. He dropped down to his knees and picked up the tail, it was Fluffy's tail, there was no doubt about it.

The young male cougar that left the Newtown area a few days ago had traveled over twenty miles away. He'd been unsuccessful in finding anything to eat so he returned to Newtown, figuring that cats and dogs were better than nothing. The cougar had been back roaming through the watershed in and out of the housing area since last night and still hadn't found anything to eat. The watershed provided a quick escape in the event anything looked like a threat to him. It was also a quick place to disappear with his prey once he found something. It offered plenty of cover and privacy to consume his meal, undetected.

He was getting desperate and now the human was walking right under his tree. Any sign of weakness in an animal or a person sent a primal signal to the cougar that it was prey. He watched as Frank walked, tired and a little unsteady past the tree. When the man was about twenty feet away the cougar dropped down to the ground and followed him, like a whisper in the wind.

When Frank fell to his knees it was the sign the cougar was waiting for. With one twenty foot leap the cougar was on him. It clamped his huge jaws on the back of his head and put a claw into his shoulder. Frank tried to move, but the cougar pulled his claw down and flipped him over. It then clamped his massive jaws down on Frank's throat and his eyes bulged out as he struggled to get the cat off of him. The cougar's bite crushed his windpipe, making it impossible for Frank to scream. It also cut off his ability to breath. As Frank tried to fight the cat, it shook its head from side to side and literally tore his throat out. Ripping and tearing, he began to feed. In two hours, when he finished feeding he covered the body with leaves and branches to keep other animals from eating it and returned to his same tree to sleep for the night.

Later that night a pack of coyotes, mother, father and five three-month-old pups, were traversing through the watershed in search of food, prey had been scarce for them too. They went into the housing development about three o'clock in the morning and began to roam around the houses in search of food. Coyotes are smart hunters, especially in packs. When they find a dog in a yard they send the pups in to play with the dog. They make friends and then the pups draw the dog out into the woods, where the rest of the pack lay in wait. Once the dog is lured away from people the whole pack attacks the dog and eats it. The coyotes were unsuccessful in finding anything in the housing area and returned to the watershed to hunt for other animals. As they moved around the woods, sniffing and hunting they came across the cougar's cache. They quickly uncovered it and devoured most of what remained of Frank's body, in many places, licking the skeleton clean.

The cougar lay in a tree nearby, staying close to his cache. He heard the coyotes coming through the woods and saw the coyotes uncovering its cache. The cougar could easily take one coyote, but seven wasn't a good idea. Coyotes are good pack hunters, with that many of them they could surround the cougar and attack from all sides. The cougar watched and listened as his food supply disappeared.

Photo by Lee Dygert

15

The Logan boys spent most of the previous day catching up on some much needed sleep. Today they were back on their usual routine and after Buck got the family on their way he decided to do his jog in the morning. They were calling for rain in the afternoon and jogging in the rain wasn't as much fun. He still wasn't feeling quite up to par after the lake trip survival experience, so the jog was slow. In fact, some of it was more of a fast walk. He was walking past Frank's place and noticed that the front sprinkler was still on. He thought that it had been on when he drove past last night and it seemed to be in the same place. The water was now running down the street as far as he could see. It sure looked like it could have been on since yesterday. He went up to the front door and rang the bell, but there was no answer so he went around to the back of the house to look for Frank. The shed door was open and the lawn mower was outside next to the shed. It looked like it had been left outside over night. Knowing how fastidious Frank was that seemed out of character for him. Perhaps something went wrong, or maybe he felt bad and was inside.

Buck went back around to the front of the house and tried the doorknob. It was unlocked so he put his head in and yelled.

"Frank!" There was no answer. He figured he knew Frank well enough to go in and look around. Who knows, he might be sick, had a stroke, or fallen and needed help. He went around the whole house, but didn't find Frank. The bed was neatly made and nothing looked out of order or unusual.

Buck went back outside and took another walk around the whole house and through the garage, but there was still no sign of Frank. His car was in the garage so it was likely he was around somewhere. He went over to the shed and looked around and saw shoe prints in the damp ground of a trail going into the woods so he began to follow the trail.

It didn't take long for him to find Frank's skeleton. That was about all that was left. He was sure it was Frank because he recognized the torn tattered clothes and the old shoes next to the skeleton. The skeleton was pretty much licked clean. Buck came to a logical conclusion this could possibly be the work of a cougar, but how could it eat so much in such a short time? The retired ranger consultant said it'd probably happen this way. He didn't think anyone expected it to happen this fast, but the ranger said it would probably come back and when it did it would be a surprise.

Buck looked around and up into the trees for a cougar. He'd already had enough experiences with cougars this week and wasn't interested in any more. He cautiously made his way back to Frank's house, went inside, and called 9-1-1 to report his findings.

The sheriff's department cars began arriving quickly, they all wanted to get a good look at the gruesome sight. Buck took Sheriff Tate and the deputies out into the woods to Frank's skeleton. They all looked at it in amazement, thinking this thing must really be hungry because there wasn't anything left.

Sheriff Tate told one of the deputies to start taking the required information from the site. He had two go around the neighborhood to notify the people. The last two deputies were told to start patrolling the area looking for the cougar.

"Get on the radio and notify everyone immediately if you see it."

Sheriff Tate went to his car and radioed his office to connect him to the mayor. When she answered the phone, Sheriff Tate explained his findings and told her he intended to get Mr. Woods to the site.

"Yes, do it as fast as possible."

Sheriff Tate then told the dispatcher to get Mr. Woods on the phone and to notify the coroner to get out to the site for an investigation.

The dispatcher placed the call. "Woods here," he said as he answered his cell phone.

"Standby one, I'm patching you through to Sheriff Tate," the dispatcher responded.

"Mr. Woods this is Sheriff Tate. We have a dead body, actually a skeleton, that we've just discovered. It's a very recent death. The victim appears to have been killed by and animal, possible a cougar. Can you get over here as soon as possible?"

"As it turns out I'm not far away at the moment. I have an assistant and two dogs with me. Give me your location and we should be there in about fifteen minutes."

Sheriff Tate gave him the address and terminated the connection. He then told the deputy on desk duty to notify the mayor that Mr. Woods was on his way and that he was going back to the body. If he needed to be contacted, use his portable radio frequency.

About eleven thirty the coroner and Mr. Woods arrived at the scene. They both took a scrutinizing look at the area. There were teeth marks on the bones indicating that some kind of animal had definitely eaten the body. The time frame puzzled them though, if what Buck told them was accurate. Buck had seen Frank in the yard two days ago when they came home from the hospital. The Sheriff concurred with Buck that it was probably Frank. Analysis of the skeleton would be needed for proof though. The Sheriff asked Mr. Woods, "Do you think that a cougar did this?"

"I'm not sure," Woods responded. "There appears to be teeth marks on some of the bones. That's a little unusual for cougars. They normally use their raspy tongue to remove the flesh from the bone. That does not leave teeth marks. It sure looks like an animal was responsible for this though. It appears to be very fresh. That being the case there would have to be multiple animals involved."

"The ground around here is too hard packed to find any footprints and there isn't any scat in the area to confirm what it could be. One cougar couldn't have eaten a whole man and left a skeleton this clean in one or two days, that's for certain. I'm going to the truck to get the dogs and we'll see what they think."

The dogs were very excited.

"The dogs have a strong scent," Woods reported.

The Sheriff gave Mr. Woods a verbal contract to

track down and kill whatever animal had killed and eaten
Frank.   He didn't want any more of the town citizens
being eaten on his watch.

Woods and his assistant went back to the truck and
got their equipment and his nine-millimeter pistol.
Usually, Woods would wait for the rest of his team, but
under these circumstances, the situation called for
immediate action. The trail was hot now and waiting
wouldn't be a good idea. The Sheriff agreed to send two
of his deputies with Mr. Woods to track down the cougar.

Woods took the dogs over to the skeleton to sniff
around and then let them go. They took off at a run
following the scent, the scent of the coyotes. The hunting
dogs were trained to follow the scent of cougars, bears or
coyotes. The dogs couldn't tell Mr. Woods that it was
coyote scent they were following, but under the
circumstances they didn't know exactly what happened or
exactly what they were tracking. The dogs only knew it
was some type of animal they'd been trained to track.

By three o'clock, the commotion in Frank's backyard
had calmed down.   Buck had gone home around two
o'clock when he figured he couldn't do anything else to
help.   The skeleton was picked up and taken to the
coroner's office for further examination.   The Sheriff
returned to his office to monitor Mr. Woods' progress via
the two-way radio. The rest of the onlookers went back to
their business.

The pack of coyotes had an eight-hour lead on the
dog team and were well into the forest before the dogs got
started. As the team tracked the culprits they went deeper
and deeper into the forest. After about two miles, Mr.
Woods began finding scat. It was clearly coyote scat and
he was puzzled.   It would be highly unusual, almost
unheard of, for a coyote or even a pack of coyotes, to kill
an adult man. However, if the pack came across a man

who was already dead, they would eat it. Mr. Woods was puzzled by the findings, but the dogs were in hot pursuit. They needed to track it or them down and would try to sort out the particulars later.

As they followed the dogs they came out of the forest into a clear area where there was an old log cabin and a big old barn.   Apparently, they had left the National Forest area and were now on private property, Walter Johnson's property. Mr. Woods wanted to get permission from the owner to cross their land in pursuit with the dogs. He ran over to the cabin and found the door was open, so he knocked on the door casing.

"Hello, anybody home?" No answer. He put his head inside and knocked on the door again.

"Hello, is anyone here?" There was still no answer.

He went inside and immediately smelled the pungent odor of cat urine. The kitchen looked like there was someone living there so he went into the bedroom. It also looked used, the bed was unmade, and the closet door was open. The closet revealed a full side of men's clothes, mostly older ones and only two very old dresses on the other side. There was a variety of shoes and boots on the floor of the closet, but they were all men's. As he walked back through the kitchen he saw it, scat on the kitchen floor.   Unmistakably cougar scat and he smelled the telltale odor of cat urine. He looked around and saw a dried stain on the wall at the corner. He went over to examine it, definitely cat urine and there was too much for it to be a housecat. He went outside and looked in the barn, nothing unusual there.

He keyed his two way radio, "Newtown Sheriff this is team leader."

"Team leader, this is Newtown Sheriff."

"We're at an old log cabin northwest of Newtown, adjacent to what looks like a shopping center." As he was talking he walked around the house and noticed long deep scratch marks on the window casing, definitely left by a cougar sharpening its claws.

"There doesn't appear to be anyone here, but there was definitely a cougar here. The front door was open when we arrived and there has been a cougar inside the house. I recommend you send someone over here to investigate. We'll continue on following the dogs. They have a strong scent. Out"

"Team leader, this is Newtown Sheriff, sounds like old man Johnson's place. We'll send a couple of deputies over there to check it out. Keep us informed of your progress. There's news people all over the place at the city hall parking lot. The mayor was just in here to get an update on what happening, and she's not a happy camper. Out"

The young male cougar moved away from the kill site immediately after the coyotes left and was lying up in an old tree. This seemed like a good spot, watching the elementary school bus come down the street. The big yellow bus came at the same time every day, once it stopped, all these little people jumped out. He was ready for another meal and watched intently as the bus pulled to a stop almost directly beneath him. The door opened and they began to pop out, making a lot of noise.

Sally May was fumbling around in the bus and was the last one to disembark. She had a cold and wasn't feeling very good. As she got off the bus she stumbled and fell. That was all it took for the cougar, a sign of weakness instinctively triggering the attack mechanism. The bus pulled away and the cougar dropped out of the tree right next to Sally May. He clamped its massive jaws down on her shoulder and began to drag her away. This was easy prey, no hurry in killing it.

Sally May screamed, at the pain in her shoulder. She looked over her shoulder straight into the cougar's eyes and quickly fainted.

Some of the parents were there to meet their children as they got off the bus. The older children chafed at a parent being near the bus when they got off, so there were only two mothers there today and they were both across the street. One of them noticed something big drop out of the tree just in time to see the cougar grab Sally May and drag her off into the bushes.

The mother ran across the street yelling, "Cougar! Cougar!"

Buck was at the mailbox picking up his mail when he heard one of the mother's yelling. It didn't sound like a false alarm and he ran over to her.

"Where, what happened?"

"A cougar, over there! It took Sally May off into the woods!" she yelled in panic.

Buck ran up his driveway to his garage and yelled over his shoulder, "Go up to Sally's and call 9-1-1!"

On the inside, near the opening, he kept his garden tools. Some were propped up in the corner and some were neatly hung on the wall. Looking for the most menacing tool in the bunch, he grabbed the pitchfork. His knowledge of cougars told him that around people, they could usually be frightened off fairly easily. His experience last Monday told him to be careful.

He ran across the street to where the bus had stopped and went into the woods, carefully looking around. He followed an animal path, it seemed like a logical way for the cougar to go, and it was easy to traverse. For about two hundred yards there was only one trail, then it came to a junction. He looked down at the ground and he could see that something had been dragged in the dirt down one side, but not on the other, this seemed like the best bet. Once he noticed the drag marks it was easier to follow the trail. As he came to other junctions, he quickly picked the right way to go by looking for the drag marks.

Sally called the sheriff's department and in a panic said, "The cougar has taken my daughter. Get over here fast."

He got her address and quickly realized that all of the deputies were out chasing the cougar on the other side of town. Every deputy that wasn't on the chase with Mr. Woods was at Walter Johnson's tree farm. He called Sheriff Tate and explained the situation to him as he was using the other radio to get the extra deputies at Johnson's farm over to Sally's place.

After about fifteen minutes Buck came to an embankment with an old dirt road up above. The trail was clearly leading him to a culvert that went under the road. He went over to the entrance to the culvert, it was a cement pipe about five feet high that passed under the highway for water runoff. He looked into the pipe, it was dark inside and it took a minute for his eyes to adjust to the dim light. As his eyes adjusted, he saw the cougar crouched down facing the other direction about halfway through the pipe. He could see Sally May's legs under the cougar and apparently it didn't hear his approach because it didn't move. It looked like the cougar was resting, probably tired from dragging Sally May for such a distance.

Buck thought, 'if I can frighten the cougar into going out the other side, I can bring Sally May back out this side.' He slammed the pitchfork against the side of the culvert making a loud, high pitched, metallic ringing sound and yelled as loud as he could at the same time. The cougar jumped up and turned around. Its eyesight was better than Buck's and hissed a menacing hiss. It stood directly over Sally May, protecting its meal. Buck realized this wasn't going to work so he started into the culvert, brandishing the pitchfork in front of him, shaking it and yelling at the same time. The cougar stood its ground, guarding its meal.

Buck continued his advance thinking this isn't the best place to mount an attack. The cougar clearly had the advantage, as he needed to hunch over to get through the pipe. To get a better grip in case the cougar attacked he put his other hand on the pitchfork handle and turned the fork so the tines were facing up, that seemed like the best position. Too bad they were curved tines, straight ones would be best under the circumstances. The good news was they were very sharp and he advanced with caution.

The cougar took Sally May's blood stained shoulder in its massive jaws and began backing up, dragging Sally May's limp body. It kept a steady eye on Buck as it backed out of the culvert. It continued to back up until it was about five feet out of the pipe. Buck slammed the pitchfork against the side of the culvert producing a loud metallic ringing sound. When he was about to exit the culvert he slammed the tines against the cement wall again, lunging toward the cat. Then, it crouched down and sprang upward, disappearing from his sight. Buck couldn't believe it. He cautiously went to the end of the tunnel and carefully looked around from side to side, then above the culvert bank, listening intently, but there was no hint of the cougar. Buck stood still, listening, nothing. He quickly looked down at Sally May to assess her injuries. Her clothes were heavily blood stained. If she was still alive he needed to act quickly or she would bleed to death.

Slowly he moved forward, looking all around, pitchfork held in front of him. When he got next to Sally May he realized he was out in the open, exposed, and vulnerable to an attack. He looked up at the road above the culvert one more time, but the cat was not there. He bent down holding the pitchfork in his right hand as he put his other hand on Sally May's forehead. It was cool, but not cold. He put his forefinger on her throat, he was sure he could feel a pulse, but it was very weak.

He put his hand back on her forehead and asked "Sally May, can you hear me?"

She opened her left eye slightly and said in a small voice, "My shoulder hurts."

That was all the incentive Buck needed to go on. He wasn't sure if she had internal injuries or head, neck or spine injuries. He knew for certain he had to get her back before she bled to death and he couldn't tend to her injuries here with the cougar's position unknown. Looking around to make sure he didn't see the cougar he picked Sally May up with his left arm and gingerly placed her on his left shoulder, still holding the pitchfork in his right hand. The culvert was the best and fastest way to get back to help. He backed up to the culvert, looked around and continued backing up through the culvert, intently watching the opening. About halfway through it hit him, the cougar could come around from behind. He looked behind him, but there was nothing. He realized that if the cougar attacked from behind while he was still in the culvert, he wouldn't be able to turn the pitchfork around. The diameter of the culvert was less than the length of the pitchfork. The handle of the pitchfork was better than nothing, but not nearly as good a weapon as the business end.

He finally reached the other end and backed out of the culvert. He breathed a sigh of relief that he was out.

He started to stand straight up when he heard it. The cougar let out a bloodcurdling scream as it lunged off the side of the embankment. Buck had no time to think, instinctively he raised the pitchfork with his right hand, pushing back hard on the base of the handle to lodge it in the mud, he pulled Sally May in closer to his chest. The cougar landed right on him, face to face, its three-inch long fangs snarling from its massive powerful jaws. Its front claws hit Buck's shoulders and pulled the razor sharp claws down his forearms, pulling Sally May off his shoulder. The cougar let out another scream and menacingly stood there, it's hind legs on the ground. It had impaled itself on the pitchfork right through the chest.

Buck couldn't have placed the pitchfork better if he had planned it that way.

The cat made a final lunge toward Buck, pushing the pitchfork tines deeper into its chest. The cougar tried to pull back to relieve the pain, but Buck pushed forward, keeping the pitchfork in the cougar. The cat was strong, but the pain kept it from using its full force. Buck gave another strong push, forcing the cat back further and pushing the pitchfork through its lungs and through the stomach wall. Blood began to foam out of its mouth, the snarl fading, its body twitching, near death. Buck stood there staring into the cougar's face, thinking, today was his lucky day. He remembered the fight they heard between the cougar and the bear last week. Yes, today was his lucky day.

His arms burned like they were on fire and he let go of the pitchfork. Looking at his arms he realized he needed some medical attention too, but Sally May was more important, he had to get her back so they could get her to the hospital. He picked her up in both arms even though his arms burned as he headed back toward home. When he emerged from the woods the sheriff's car was just pulling up. There were about fifty people standing

around and came forward to assist as the sheriff called for
an ambulance on the car radio. Two more deputy
sheriff's cars arrived.

Sally took Sally May out of his arms and hugged her.
"Sally May!"

Sally May opened her eyes and said, "Mommy."
They both began to cry.

Buck told the deputies where to find the cougar. Two
of them pulled their pistols out and went off into the
woods to ensure it was dead. Buck lay down on the grass,
exhausted. One of the deputies came over to him and
began putting some gauze on the deep gashes the cougar's
claws had made on both of his forearms.

In about twenty minutes Eric and Rob drove into the
driveway and saw all the commotion. They joined the
crowd to see what was going on as two deputies emerged
from the woods carrying the dead cougar.

"Cool," Eric said, admiring the dead animal.

Rob analyzed the dead cougar from head to tail,
taking in every detail. "It sure has some big, powerful
looking paws," he observed.

They saw Buck lying on the grass and went over to
him.

"I've changed my mind. I don't want to go deer
hunting. I want to go cougar hunting."

Buck pulled the gauze off of one arm, exposing the
deep gashes for them to see. "This is what a cougar can
do to you, if you're lucky."

Eric's eyes grew large, "Well, maybe not today."

EPILOGUE

As civilization across the United States expands, it moves into the formerly unpopulated areas, former farmland, forest land and other undeveloped land, into the habitat of cougars and other wild animals. We are faced with a dilemma. How do we find a suitable solution to this evolution? Humans and cougars cannot cohabitant. Cougars are carnivores; they will eat any meat; deer, porcupines, skunks and humans.

Harold P. Danz, an authority on cougars and cougar behavior, states at the beginning of his latest book, "Softer than the light summer breeze upon your cheek, quieter than the sound of a snowflake's fall, the cougar strides through the forest and the countryside. One of the most successful of animal predators in the Americas, has the cougar now become a threat to humans?" Cougar!, Harold P. Danz, 1999.

"Under certain circumstances they can and will continue to present real, and not only potential, threat to human life. This is not because of any implied or inherent viciousness of the cougar's, but primarily because of its unpredictability and confounding, enigmatic presence." Cougar!, Harold P. Danz, 1999, p. 179.

The cougar, also known as puma, mountain lion, or panther is an efficient predator, one of the most efficient predators on the face of the earth. It has the most voracious appetite of any predator in the United States. An adult cougar can weigh well over two hundred pounds, about ten to twenty times the size of a house cat.

The largest documented cougar was killed by J. R. Patterson, a government hunter, outside Hillside, AZ, in March, 1917. It weighed 276 pounds, after the intestines had been removed.

Cougars can meow, hiss and growl. They make whistling noises to greet another cougar. Cougars, like house cats, can also purr. Since a cougar is twenty times the size of a house cat, the purr is much louder.

Cougars hold the world record for the longest jump for a land animal. A cougar in the wild was filmed jumping sixty feet down from a tree. Cougars can jump up twenty feet into a tree. From a run, a cougar can jump thirty feet ahead, from a standing still position, it can jump about twenty feet.

Cougars are voracious carnivores. There are a few exceptions, they have been observed eating insects, such as grasshoppers. They will also eat grass occasionally. The grass acts as a natural laxative to purge any intestinal parasites or intestinal blockages. In the 1800's, the cougar was also known as the "Deer Tiger" because of its propensity to kill and eat deer. Deer are the primary food source for cougars, they will kill a deer about every two to fifteen days, if there is a sufficient number of deer in its territory. After the kill, the cougar will feed until it is full, a cougar can eat twenty to thirty pounds of meat at a single feeding. It will then cache, or cover the carcass with twigs, leaves and dirt, coming back daily until it has eaten all of the carcass or until the meat has gone bad. If the cougar catches another animal eating its cache, it will kill and eat that animal. Cougars usually stay near their cache to keep an eye on it.

Cougars can have up to six kittens in a litter, but on average give birth to two or three. Usually the mother cougar will give birth to the kittens in a den. The kittens will stay in the den until they are about two months old. During those first two months the mother cougar will leave the kittens in the den to hunt for food. The mother cougar may be gone for up to thirty hours when hunting for food. When the kittens reach about two to four months old they come out of the den to begin learning to hunt from the mother, they will then travel with the mother, looking for prey. Cougar kittens begin to eat meat around six weeks old and they are usually completely weaned at about three months old. The kittens may stay with the mother for up to two years.

A female cougar will not go into heat, estrus, while it has kittens. Once the mother disperses the kittens it will go into estrus about every three weeks until it becomes pregnant again. The heat period lasts seven to eight days, during which time the female cougar screams a bloodcurdling scream that travels long distances. Cougar territories are large, as much as ten by thirty miles, and cougars do not share areas with other adult cougars, the female must announce her estrus loud enough to draw in a male cougar.

If a male cougar comes into the mother cougar's territory it will attempt to kill the kittens. By killing the kittens the female will go back into heat again soon. For this reason a mother cougar will become very aggressive when a male cougar comes into her area when she has kittens, she will drive the male away to save her kittens.

Cougars will not share habitat areas. If a cougar enters another's occupied habitat there will be a fight to the death, with the victor eating the looser.

In the early to mid 1900's, cougars were considered dangerous predators. During this period cattle and sheep ranching were both in a substantial growth phase. Much of the time the ranches were near cougar habitat, consequently, some of the farm animals were killed and eaten by cougars. In some cases, cougars would enter a pen of sheep at night and kill every sheep in the pen, even though it would only eat one. The ranchers wanted all cougars killed and they developed plans to rid an area up to 150 miles from ranches, of all cougars. Many of the western states put a bounty on cougars to reduce the population. Some cougar hunters would kill as many as twenty a day. There are pictures in some older towns that show cougars stacked up like cordwood.

The author first experienced the cougar problem while on a fishing trip to Kernville, California in the early 1980's. The Kernville newspaper stated that a cougar had killed a sheep in town at the rodeo yard the night before. The sheep was found cached the next day near the riverbed about 1/2 mile from the rodeo yard, still within town limits. When the cougar returned the next night the authorities were waiting for it. Research by the author revealed that a cougar on the other side of town had killed a mule about six months before. It turned out that the cougar frequently came out of the hills into town to look for food. A trip to the town museum revealed many pictures of cougar hunts for bounty in the 1930-1950's. In one picture, the bounty hunter had piled up twenty-three cougar carcasses. At the current time, there are no bounties on cougar in the United States that the author is aware of.

Some states, including Washington and Oregon, have outlawed hunting cougars and bears with dogs. This is happening at a time when the deer population is on the rise. Since cougars and bears both eat deer, the population of these predatory animals will likely increase also. This new policy may also exacerbate the predator population to increase.

Cougars tend to be nocturnal, although they do travel and hunt in the daytime. Cougars are similar to house cats in that they sleep about 20 hours per day. They are very difficult, but not impossible, to hunt without dogs.

The laws to outlaw hunting with dogs are usually voted in by the public. These new policies will start a new trend of cougar population growth, which will take time to evolve. It is highly likely that there will be an increase in cougar sightings, encroachment into housing areas, and more human fatalities.

The result will likely be the development of a new industry in trapping or killing errant cougars and bears. If the problem becomes too common, the public will eventually vote back hunting cougars and bears with dogs. This is by far the most cost effective method for the taxpayer, since hunters do it for sport and food at no cost to the taxpayer. It is probably the most efficient method of keeping these animals in check with nature.

Cougars tend to be shy reclusive animals, rarely seen by humans until the 1990's. Because of this, the mysterious species was misunderstood. Dr. Maurice Hornocker began cougar research in the 1960's, and is credited with the first documented scientific research about the cougar. He has done extensive research on cougars throughout the western United States, Canada, and has done big cat research in Russia.

The author's research indicates that a male human is just as likely to be attacked as a female human. In addition, a study of the number of attacks on humans for the past thirty reveals an almost equal number of attacks on children as it does for adults, using sixteen years as the cutoff age in determining the difference between adults and children. There was no time of the year which seemed to have more attacks. They essentially occurred any time of the year. There was only one recurring similar factor in cougar attacks. The victim was almost always alone. In the attacks on children, nearly all occurred when the child was separated from the group.

Cougars tend to be more likely to attack when the victim is running away, jogging, bicycling, crouching down or even riding a snow mobile. Documented cases where a cougar approached people indicate that if the person looks straight into the eyes of the cougar, it will generally leave. Cougars look for signs of weakness in their victims. When a cougar approaches a person, the person should be standing up as tall as possible and making menacing movements, like shaking the arms, any method of trying to look as big as possible. Do not bend over, such as to pick up a rock or stick. Bending over or crouching down is a sign of weakness or giving up. Cougars are fast, an attack can occur instantly on one who crouches down. A cougar can jump 20 feet in one bound. Once a cougar attacks, it is hard to get it off, if it gets a good bite on the neck on the first attack, it could be over in seconds.

Many cougar attacks have been successfully stopped by people nearby. Yelling and throwing things, especially rocks, can deter the cougar and cause it to leave the area. However, a rescuer should never touch the cougar with any part of their own body. In three cases in the past thirty years where a would be rescuer touched the cougar, the cougar turned on the rescuer and kill them.   In each case the rescuer that was killed was an adult female.

The recent work by Harold P. Danz, Cougar!, 1999, is an excellent source of information about the cougar. He has put together a tremendous amount of research in accumulating statistical information, which includes cougar attacks. The book documents over 150 cougar attacks on humans, these are only the documented attacks. Many cougar attacks on humans in the past have not been reported. Some of the attacks have been reported in local, small town newspapers, but no place else. These are virtually impossible to track down. The real number of cougar attacks is an unknown. What is important to follow is the number of cougar attacks that have occurred since 1996 to present. The number and frequency of attacks during this period have increased over the previous years. We need to study this increase to determine the trends that are developing and how the cougar population expansion is likely to affect the areas populated by humans.

OTHER FACT BOOKS ABOUT COUGARS:

Robert H. Busch, <u>The Cougar Almanac</u>, 1996
Harold P. Danz, <u>Cougar!</u>, 1999
*Hornocker, Maurice, PhD, <u>Track of the Cat</u>, 1997
Karen McCall and Jim Duthere, <u>Cougar</u>, 1992
Dennis L. Olson, <u>Solitary Spirits Cougars</u>, 1996